MY LITTLE PHONY

MY LITTLE PHONY

A CLIQUE NOVEL BY
LISI HARRISON

poppy

LITTLE, BROWN AND COMPANY
New York   Boston

Poppy

Little, Brown and Company
Hachette Book Group
237 Park Avenue, New York, NY 10017
For more of your favorite series, go to www.pickapoppy.com

First Edition: August 2010

Poppy is an imprint of Little, Brown and Company.
The Poppy name and logo are trademarks of Hachette Book Group, Inc.

Cover design by Andrea C. Uva
Cover photos by Roger Moenks
Author photo by Gillian Crane

alloyentertainment
Produced by Alloy Entertainment
151 West 26th Street, New York, NY 10001

ISBN: 978-0-316-08444-4

10 9 8 7 6 5 4 3 2 1
CWO
Printed in the United States of America

It takes a village. Thank you, fellow villagers. This is for you.

"I love getting stoned," Massie Block sighed happily from one of the three massage tables set up in her family's barn-spa. Heated stones lay on her back, radiating warmth through her entire body like she'd just downed three soy caramel lattes.

"If we were in school right now, we'd be in third-period French," Kristen Gregory mumbled through the face hole in her massage table. The stones lined her spine like stegosaurus plates.

"*J'adore* snow days," trilled Alicia Rivera, lying on her back at the end of the row, her long, dark brown hair fanned out behind her head. Her masseuse, Amber, spritzed her with Evian mineral water.

"*Oui, oui,*" Kristen agreed.

"*Woof!*" Bean chimed in from her own mini massage bed.

"Tatiana, how do you say 'snow day' in Russian?" Massie asked innocently.

"Shhhhh," hissed Tatiana. "Talking eees naht relaaacksing. Jash theenk abut a bee-yoo-ti-ful snoh-flok."

Tatiana claimed to be "frahmm RAH-shah," but Massie had a feeling her accent was about as real as Heidi Pratt's new body. Not that it mattered. Her hands were pure gold. And with all those rocks lined up on her back, Massie felt like the black diamond stretch bracelet on her Christmas list: relaxed, beautiful, and almost a million bucks.

Massie turned her head to look out the barn's sophisticated yet rustic plate-glass windows. It had snowed more than two feet the night before. The patios were dusted with shimmery powder, and the trees sparkled in the early December sun. It looked as though the MAC fairy had sprinkled pearly White Frost eye shadow over the entire Block estate and then blown it a kiss with her Sugarrimmed Dazzleglass–coated lips.

"CLAAAAAAAAAAAAIRE!" Layne Abeley's gravelly voice boomed from outside.

"AHHHHH! I've been hit!"

CRASH!

Outside, a body slammed against the barn wall, and the spa shook. A high-pitched giggle followed.

"Eh-ma-annoying!" Massie flipped over, her heated stones tumbling to the floor. Her ex-BFF, Claire Lyons, had been squealing and giggling with her new friends all afternoon. Leave it to Claire to find the only ninth-grade girls who thought snowball fights were more fun than high school gossip. It was a total waste of an upgrade.

"Eeeen-hayel the soo-theeng ah-rom-ah," Tatiana instructed, guiding Massie back down to the table and replacing the rocks. Spicy steam startled Massie's pores as the masseuse kneaded the tension from her shoulders. But it was a lost cause. No amount of eucalyptus-infused steam could ease the pain of Claire ditching the Pretty Committee for *Layme* Abeley and two fourteen-year-old theater geeks.

Suddenly, the barn's wooden door flew open. Dylan Marvil rushed in, along with an arctic blast of air. Snowflakes speckled the back of her black cashmere coat like dandruff. Her white-mittened hands grasped the handles of a dozen brightly colored shopping bags, and her cheeks were as red as her hair.

"Where've you been?" Alicia sat up, pressing a fluffy green towel against her C-cups.

"Shooooooooooooooopppping!" Dylan burped. She set down a cardboard tray full of venti Starbucks hot chocolates and wiped her brown-stache with the back of her mitten. A cocoa-colored skid mark cut across the cashmere. "Ooops!" she shrugged. "Good thing I got a new pair. I cleaned out Neiman's, Juicy, and Michael Kors. Snow-day shopping is the best."

"Point-t-t-t," Alicia agreed through chattering teeth.

Massie pressed a button on a sleek silver remote. A second later, the electric fire in the stone fireplace ignited.

Dylan tossed her stained mittens into the hungry flames and then shook her crimson locks.

"Nice lice, Dyl!" Kristen cackled. Alicia snickered, her freshly manicured toes dangling just above the heated tile floor.

As Dylan whirled back toward them, her Brazilian blowout whipped around her face. "Don't even joke! When Megan Lambert got lice, her friends scattered like roaches in a Raid storm." She stuck her butt out to warm it in the fire's glow.

"Let's see what you got." Massie stood, and once again the pile of rocks cascaded off her warm back and crashed to the ground. Bean bolted under the glass coffee table.

"Nyyyetttttt!" Tatiana let out a yelp as one of the rocks bounced against her toe. "Off! Off!" she insisted, waving Kristen and Alicia to their feet. With a grimace, she nodded at the other masseuses, who quickly folded up their tables, packed up their oils, picked up their rocks, and followed her out into the cold afternoon.

"*Danke* very much," Massie called after them sweetly, putting on a fluffy white robe.

The three women responded by slamming the barn door shut.

"Isn't *danke* German?" Kristen giggled.

"Oh, whatevs," Massie shrugged. "They dan-kare." She padded over to Dylan's pile of bags and pulled out a baby blue cashmere hat with earflaps and tassels. It looked like something Kuh-laire would wear. With a wince, she dropped it back in the bag. "You really did buy *everything*."

"I maxed out my card," Dylan admitted. "But it was totally worth it. I got open-toed booties in faux leopard *and* faux cheetah."

"Ohhh," Alicia whine-pouted. "I'm faux jealous." Her shoulders were covered with spiderweb-like indentations from lying down on the massage table. "I can't buy anything right now. My parents told me they would send me to the Spanish Riviera for a week if I didn't shop from Thanksgiving to Christmas." She buried her nose inside Dylan's Saks bag and inhaled a Ralph Lauren sweater-coat. "Ahhhh! It's better than new puppy smell."

Bean lifted her little black head and growled.

"She was only kidding, B," Massie assured her pup, applying a coat of Pineapple Spice Glossip Girl to the pug's mouth. The pug licked it off and then sneezed. "My parents would *never* shop-block me."

"Must be nice," Kristen said with a frown.

"It is," Massie beamed.

THUNK!

THUNK!

THUNK!

Three snowballs hit the windows, slithering down the glass like snot. A peal of high-pitched laughter followed the barrage. Kristen and Alicia threw on thick robes, and the four girls raced to the windows.

Claire, dressed in a My Little Pony cap and a bright red puffy coat, was pelting snowballs at Layne and their new friends—a willowy blonde and a petite brunette.

"They're ruining my snow!" Massie stared at the once pristine yard, which was now covered with LBR boot prints.

"Cheap footwear leaves the most horrible tracks," Dylan sighed. "Like the abdominal snowman."

"You mean *abominable* snowman," Kristen corrected.

Dylan pinched some snow off her fluffy hood and dropped it onto Kristen's head. "Takes one to know one."

"Ew, lice!" Alicia giggled, pointing at Kristen's scalp. "Let's go before we catch it," she joked, backing away.

Kristen shook her blond hair in Alicia's face.

"Ahhhhhh!"

Massie drew an *X* on the foggy window, her finger squeaking on the pane. "It's too bad we can't give Claire lice. Maybe her ah-nnoying friends would leave."

THUNK.

THUNK.

THUNK!

The girls jumped back as another round of snowballs smacked into the barn.

Todd dashed in front of the window and bowed, proud to claim responsibility for the latest round.

Massie whipped her iPhone out of her robe pocket. "Unless . . ."

"Is there a lice app?" Kristen asked, twisting her damp hair into a sloppy bun.

"I wish," Massie smirked, her breath clouding the window as she coaxed her brain into constructing the ultimate plan— a plan that would accomplish her sinister goal without implicating her sinister mind. Seven breath clouds later, she had it. And sent an urgent text to Claire's younger brother.

Massie: Come 2 the barn ay-sap. Impt.

Bwoop.

The message had been sent. Seconds later, Todd and his best friend, Tiny Nathan, appeared in the doorway. Todd looked like a freckled Buzz Lightyear in his puffy white-and-green snowsuit. Nathan resembled a poo in his three-sizes-too-big brown snow pants and matching hooded coat.

Todd sniffled. "You wanna join our team?" He pulled off his hood. His orange hair was spiked with sweat. "We're called Big Balls."

Nathan giggled. And then Todd giggled. And then Nathan giggled some more.

"No, this is nawt about joining your—"

Massie's iPhone buzzed.

Kristen: ??? R U doing?
Alicia: ??? Does this have 2 do w lice?
Dylan: Ha! Big balls. ☺
Massie: Quit bugging me. ☺ Trust me.

Massie reached for the pack of Mango Surf–flavored Orbit sticking out of Dylan's purse and popped a piece in her mouth. She bit down, recalling the satisfying flavor that squishing the competition usually left in her mouth. "I just learned a new massage technique that I'm dying to try on someone. It's supposed to increase scalp circulation and prevent hair from sweating." Massie waved away the imaginary smell coming from Todd's head.

Alicia and Kristen exchanged confused looks. Dylan snatched the pack of gum out of Massie's hand and stuffed four pieces in her mouth.

"Why didn't you try it out on Kristen, then?" Tiny Nathan pointed out.

"This isn't sweat." Kristen smoothed the wet hair on top of her head. "It's melted snow, okay?" She flashed Dylan a *thanks a lot* look.

Dylan blew her a glossy *you're welcome* kiss.

Todd's eyes darted between the two girls in confusion.

"So whaddaya say?" Massie asked Todd, putting the attention back where it belonged. "Wanna give it a try?"

"Oh. Okay." Todd hopped up onto the couch and lay down. Tiny Nathan promptly pulled out his cell phone and started angling for a photo.

Kristen shrugged her athletic shoulders. Alicia finger-combed her dark locks to glossy perfection. And Dylan peeled a flattened gum-bubble off the tip of her nose.

Massie's friends were the best that Octavian Country Day had to offer. Still, without Claire she felt emptier than Beyoncé after the forty-day master cleanse. But when betas defected to other crews, alphas didn't beg them to come back. They drove the betas further away. And if a little brother got hurt in the process, so be it.

"Here I go." Massie held her breath, stuck her hand into Todd's matted locks, and gingerly began rubbing his head. Who knew when he'd last washed it? She made a mental note to Purell before eating.

"I can feel it working," Todd muttered into the ecru linen cushion. After a few minutes, his breath became regular and heavy.

Dylan ran her hands through her hair the same way Massie was running hers through Todd's. Alicia elbowed her.

"What?" Dylan asked, her red brows rising. "Todd said it was working."

Kristen inched closer to Massie and mouthed, *What are you doing?*

Watch, Massie mouthed back. Then she fake-coughed and "accidentally" spit her gum onto Todd's head. It disappeared inside a mass of red curls.

"Oh no!" she cried, quickly working the wad into his hair. "My gum!"

Todd's head popped up. "Whhhaa?"

Tiny Nathan looked up from his phone and burst out laughing.

Massie widened her eyes in what she hoped looked like horror—and innocence. "Ehmagawd. I'm sooo sorry."

Todd stuck his hand up and felt his sticky, artificially flavored Mango Surf–encrusted locks. "I've been gummed!"

Kristen and Dylan snorted back giggles. Alicia tightened the belt of her robe.

"It's almost the same color as your hair. Maybe you should just leave it," Tiny Nathan suggested. "You could stick stuff to it, like paper clips and things."

Todd felt around the back of his head for the gum clump. "True."

Massie shook her head vigorously. "No, no, no. We can't leave it there. It's dangerous. It can"—her eyes landed on Tiny Nathan—"stunt a person's growth."

In a flash, Todd sat up. His gummy hair stood up from his head like the Statue of Liberty's crown.

"Stunting is not cool," Tiny Nathan assured his friend.

"Ooookay," Massie sighed. "There's really only one thing to do." She padded to the spa bathroom and opened the medicine cabinet. Inside was the silver-plated electric razor her dad kept in the cedar-planked room. She clutched it in her Essie Mint Candy Apple–manicured hands and returned to the main room, where Kristen, Alicia, and Dylan had settled on the couch, watching Todd like he was a monkey at the zoo.

"Now, not everyone can pull off the bald look. But you have such great bone structure. . . ." She held up the shaver and slid the button up to HIGH. The buzzing sound filled the room.

Todd stared at it, wide-eyed. "You want to *shave my head*?"

"No," Massie nodded seriously. "I *have* to."

The PC gasped. Todd's mouth hung slightly slack. Tiny Nathan took out his cell phone and pressed RECORD.

"Think about it. Bald men are so . . ." She looked at her friends for help.

"Hawt!" Alicia added quickly. "Like, look at Bruce Willis."

"Isn't he dead?" Dylan asked.

Alicia shrugged.

"Britney Spears did it," Kristen pointed out.

"So did Mr. Potato Head!" Dylan added helpfully.

Massie clicked to the Mirror app on her iPhone and held it up for Todd. "Think about how tough you'll look."

Todd looked at Massie and blinked. For a second she

thought he was going to freak out and run screaming to Mrs. Lyons. But then a huge grin spread over his face.

"And I'll be so much more aerodynamic!"

Tiny Nathan ran over and gave Todd a high five. "We can beat our luge time!"

Massie's high-glossed lips curved into a Cheshire cat grin. She held the buzzing shaver out in front of her. "Ready?"

Bean darted under the couch.

Todd nodded and sat down on a bamboo stool.

Kristen's jaw dropped.

Dylan let out a shocked belch.

Alicia twirled her diamond studs at top speed.

With one last glance at her friends, Massie lowered the blade. A tendril of bright red hair fluttered to the floor like an autumn leaf. And then another, and another. The buzzing blades mowed easily through the orange glob of gum. She carved a path right down the middle of his scalp. Then she made another path right next it, first on the left, and then another on the right. More and more hair dropped down onto Todd's skinny shoulders and then onto the camel-colored leather massage table.

"Looks like a motocross track," Tiny Nathan marveled, lifting his camera.

Alicia covered her eyes.

Massie pictured each tuft of hair as one of Claire's new friends. And with each strand she lopped off, she felt more and more like the Queen of Hearts, cutting off traitors' heads in the name of control.

"Done," she announced triumphantly a few minutes later, when Todd's head was shinier than a new pair of patent-leather Choos.

Todd hopped off the stool and hurried toward the mirror opposite the fireplace. He sucked in his cheeks, unzipped his snowsuit, and popped the insulated collar. "You're right," he nodded at his reflection. "I *do* have a beautifully shaped skull." He winked at his reflection, then rubbed the top of his head.

The Pretty Committee giggled into their eucalyptus-scented palms. They weren't privy to the intricate details of Massie's plan but were entertained by its execution nonetheless.

"Let's hit that luge course again!" shouted Tiny Nathan. He punched his tiny fist in the air.

"Wait!" Massie stopped Todd by the door. "It's too cold to go out without hair." She reached into one of Dylan's shopping bags and took out the baby blue cashmere Claire hat.

"Hey," Dylan protested.

Massie silenced her with a glare. Then she tore off the tag with her teeth, put the hat on Todd's head, and pulled the flaps over his ears. "Perfect. I actually got it for Kuh-laire. So make sure you give it to her when you're done."

Todd nodded that he would, the tassels bouncing around his chin. Massie picked up Dylan's tray of hot chocolates and handed them to him. "Take these, too, for her friends."

"Hey!" Dylan hissed. "Why are you doing that?"

"I'll get you another hat," Massie whisper-promised.

"I'm talking about the hot chocolates," Dylan frowned.

"Let it go," Massie narrowed her amber-colored eyes, arched one expertly plucked eyebrow, and peered out the window. Outside, Claire and her friends were innocently tending to an ill-proportioned snowman. A snowman that, thanks to Massie's ingenuity, would be on the Block Estate longer than they ever would. Because now, it was only a matter of time. . . .

She opened the barn door and sent Todd and Tiny Nathan back into the cold. The Pretty Committee shrank from the sudden chill that swept in, but Massie faced the freezing temperature, heated by the promise of victory. A promise that warmed her more than a back loaded with hot rocks ever could.

CURRENT STATE OF THE UNION

IN	OUT
Snow day	School day
Razor blades	Razor scooters
Baldheads	Redheads (Except Dylan. Her hair is Pantene-o-licious. Always was, always will be.)

The ground glistened like Frosted Mini-Wheats. Claire Lyons's fingers were purple. Her Florida-born toes had gone numb before she'd packed her first snowball. And she was fairly certain she had bang-cicles. But the sight of Cara Whitman making a snow angel, Syd Martinez shaking snow off herself like a wet dog, and Layne Abeley eating the bag of carrot noses—it warmed her like July.

Claire stuck one blue-button eye then one green-button eye into the head of her snowman and stood back to admire her work. Her creation wore a green plaid scarf, a long orange nose, and twigs for the arms, and it had a snow-and-mud soccer ball at its feet. "Look, it's a snow-*Cam*!"

Layne burst out laughing. Little carrot flakes shot out of her mouth. Claire grinned, happy that her friend appreciated the homage to her longtime crush, Cam Fisher, and his different-colored eyes.

"Very avant-garde," Cara said, tucking a loose strand of blond hair under her white mohair cloche hat. Snow covered her belted black military coat, and her L.L. Bean duck boots were soaked clean through.

"Really?" Syd crinkled her pug nose in concentration and turned up the collar on her vintage plaid coat. "I think

14

if we got a pocket watch and a hair dryer, he'd be pure Dalí."

"I think . . . your snow-Cam is about to get Van Gogh'd!" Cara pulled out Cam's blue eye and pressed it into the side of his cheek.

"Ahhhh!" Claire cried in mock horror. "Get her!"

Instantly the air was filled with flying snowballs as Claire and Syd pelted Cara. After a moment, Cara spun around and lobbed a snow grenade at Claire. She giggle-jumped for cover behind an evergreen shrub, then peeked out to see Layne and Cara shaking a branch over Syd's head.

Syd and Cara, Layne's ninth-grade community theater friends, were the smartest girls Claire knew. She'd been hanging out with them for the past three weeks and had loved every second of it. With them, it was about *culture,* not *couture,* and they cared more about fun than fashion. The four of them had gone Thanksgiving caroling and had made gingerbread cookies shaped like little Claires, Laynes, Syds, and Caras. After being under Massie's tight rein for the past year, Claire found hanging out with Syd and Cara as comfortable as her favorite Old Navy striped sweats.

She crept out from behind the bush, fixed Cam's eye, and stuck it back in place.

"Et ezz peek-ture purrrr-fect," Syd said, stealing Claire's silver ELPH out of her coat pocket. She circled the snowman, snapping pictures. "I see zis as zee centerfold for *Snowteen Magazine!*" she said. "Bee-yoo-tiful, darling! Now, give me more, more, MORE. Now, less!"

Claire laughed until her sides hurt. Syd sounded like Luc Coulotte, the artist Massie always hired to paint Bean's birthday portraits.

Another snowball whizzed past her head and hit the barn's front door. As Claire watched it fly by, her eyes landed on the four sets of designer boot prints leading to the GLU headquarters, along with a tiny pair of dog-sized tracks. Just a few weeks ago, Claire's own square boot prints would have been right there next to them. But now, even though she stood only a few feet away from her former friends, she might as well have been back in her hometown of Kissimmee, Florida.

A few weeks before, Massie had launched a mission to get Claire and the rest of the PC to upgrade from their eighth-grade crushes to crushes in ninth. And when Claire had refused, their friendship had crash-landed—hard. But it wasn't until she had caught Claire karaoke-ing with her new friends that Massie had declared war.

Since then, things between the two of them had been icier than the Blocks' swimming pool in winter. And although Claire had IM'd with Kristen, Alicia, and Dylan over Thanksgiving break, she hadn't seen the girls, been invited to a sleepover, or been awarded any gossip points. But every time she felt a pang of Massie-itis, Claire reminded herself that Massie's friendship was like an Hermès Kelly bag: rare and beautiful, but it came at way too high a price.

Claire didn't know why Massie needed to control her friends, but she did know she was sick of being bossed around. In seventh grade she probably would have gone crawling back to Massie and begged her forgiveness. But that was more than a year ago. She was already three months into eighth grade, and she planned to spend the rest of the year having no drama with her new drama friends.

"I'm going to make a snow Robert Pattinson!" Cara exclaimed, gathering piles of snow with her arms. "Just think how beee-yoooo-ti-fully he'll sparkle in the sun."

"Won't that make Doug jealous?" Syd asked. Cara's boyfriend, Doug, was the bassist in a band called Smells Like Uncle Hugh. They lip-kissed *all* the time—even in public.

"Jealousy is healthy in a relationship. When jealousy dies, passion dies," Cara said, kneeling to pack the bottom globe of the snowvamp. "I read it on the bathroom wall at school."

Claire felt a ping of jealousy herself. All the OCD bathroom walls said were things like KATIE WAS HERE or YOU'RE UGLY!

"Me-ladies!" Todd emerged from the barn, his eyes lit up like the white Christmas lights strung around the Blocks' windows. He wore a baby blue cashmere hat with earflaps and tassels. Claire frowned. The hat was totally cute but totally girly.

Tiny Nathan bobbed behind him, balancing a tray of hot chocolates. He held them out with a shaky flourish. "They're from Massie."

Claire wasn't sure what the gesture meant. Was it a truce in the name of the Christmas spirit? Or were they venti-sized cups of steaming cat pee?

Cara, Syd, and Claire inched cautiously toward the offering.

"Hmmm." Layne lifted a cup to the sun and examined the bottom. She shoved it toward Todd. "You try it first."

Tiny Nathan snort-laughed as Todd took a big gulp. "He'll do anything a girl asks him to!"

"All clear," Todd announced, licking whipped cream off his lips.

The other girls shrugged and grabbed their cups.

"Wanna know what else he'll do?" Tiny Nathan pressed.

"Not really." Claire rolled her eyes, suddenly mortified that her older friends were being forced to hang with her younger brother.

"Okayyyy," Tiny Nathan beamed. "You asked for it!"

"No, they didn't." Todd stepped back. But it was too late. Nathan jumped up like an anxious puppy and managed to grab hold of a blue tassel. He yanked twice. The hat slid off Todd's slick head and landed on the snow with a muted thud.

"You're bald!" Claire shouted.

Layne laughed so hard, hot chocolate sprayed from her nose. "You look like a Tootsie Pop."

"Thanks," Todd beamed, and then curled his fist under his chin and struck a thinking-man pose. "Massie did it. She says my skull is my best feature."

"She got that right," Syd joked.

"Even my snow-Cam has more hair than you!" Claire pointed to the little evergreen pine needles poking out the top of its head.

Layne clasped her hands together like a caroler and began to sing. "Frosssssty the bald man . . ."

"Had a jolly, shiny skull!" Cara added.

Syd threw her arm around Cara. "With an earflapped hat and a button nose and two eyes made out of . . ."

Claire stared at her transformed little brother, rage fizzing through her veins like shaken Coke Zero. But was it really anger . . . or jealousy? She used to love getting a Massie makeover.

Todd slapped his bald head. "Oh! I almost forgot." He picked the hat off the snow-covered ground. "Massie said this was for you."

Claire stared at it, her heart pounding as she went through another loop on the roller coaster that was life with Massie Block. First the hot chocolate, now this. The muscles in her hands were dying to reach out and grab the hat. To rush the barn and throw her arms around Massie and ask if the hat—a soft, stretchy cashmere—meant that they were finally going to make up. That Massie was finally going to be more flexible and let Claire make her own decisions. But her memory ordered her impulses to sit this one out. Could the girl who forbade her to eat processed sugar, hang out with Cam on a Friday night, or sit with Layne at lunch suddenly be open to change? Yeah, maybe. When Gwen Stefani tans.

Claire glanced at the barn. A familiar pair of amber eyes stared back at her from the window. Massie smiled sweetly and motioned for Claire to take the hat. Was it possible? Was Gwen was on a yacht in St. Barts slathering on the Hawaiian Tropic oil?

Stranger things have happened, she thought. *Like . . . well . . .*

Actually, Claire couldn't think of anything at the moment. She was distracted by her tingling feet, which were finally thawing with the hope of reconciliation. It had been weeks since the girls had even acknowledged each other. And a part of Claire had been numb ever since.

She studied the hat. It was soft and pale blue, the same color as her own cornflower blue eyes. She had to hand it to the alpha: When it came to knowing what looked good on people, the girl had more vision than Bausch & Lomb.

She put it on. It fit perfectly and warmed the tips of her ears. As she tied the tassels under her chin, the Massie-shaped ice block around her heart began to melt.

"It looks adorbs," Cara said.

"Totally you," Syd pronounced.

Claire grinned. She looked at the window and raised her hand to wave her thanks, but Massie was gone.

Hours later, Massie's Friday-night sleepover was in full swing. Four matching D&G sleeping bags were unfurled in flower-petal formation, with Bean's bed in the center. Belle Fleur Jasmine Verbena candles flickered on the long, white dresser. Mountains of Bliss face masks, Essie and OPI nail essentials, and yogurt-covered low-fat pretzels were strewn across the carpet. Everything was there, in its place. And at the same time, it felt like something was missing.

Massie stared out across the snowy lawn into the guest-house's warmly lit living room, where Claire and her neo-friends were engaged in some sort of sewing project. They kept throwing their heads back like they were having the most fun time in the history of Westchester. Massie swore she could hear their laughter from her sleeping bag. It was ah-nnoying squared.

"I've got it!" Dylan speed-waved her air-drying Sag Harbor Essie–polished fingernails. "Your plan is to make Claire think that Todd looks great so she'll shave her head too," she guessed.

"Opposite of right," Massie replied, zipping up Dylan's turquoise ankle booties. She examined her foot. "Cute for spring," she declared.

"Think we'll know why you shaved Todd's head by then?"

21

Kristen asked, rolling onto her back. Candlelight flickered across her flawless skin.

"You're sending Claire a warning. Like, you could shave off her power at any time." Alicia twirled a lock of hair around her index finger and mimed yanking it out of her head.

"Opposite of makes sense," Massie giggled, and then she craned her neck to spy on Claire through the window, noting with satisfaction that her former beta was still wearing the blue hat. She watched as Claire threw something at Layne's head. Layne sprang up and immediately caught whatever it was in her mouth.

"Are you trying to make the neo-friends think Todd has some sort of contagious disease?" Kristen asked.

"Something *lice* that . . ."

"Ehmagawd!" Kristen smacked Massie's back. "You want them to think Todd has *lice*!"

Massie turned away from the window and applauded. "Yayyy! Opposite of wrong!"

Alicia gasped. Dylan tossed away the floaty green boho scarf she'd been weaving through her hair. "No!" they cried out in unison.

"Oh yes." Massie grabbed her iPhone off her purple bedspread and fired off a text to Layne. "Phase two of the plan will be activated in three . . . two . . . one . . ." She tapped SEND.

Massie: Heads up! There's a louse in the house. Y do U think Todd shaved his head? Make sure Claire

doesn't wear Todd's blue hat. Sleep tight. Don't let the
head bugs bite! /\O/\

"Massie, that wasn't very lice," Kristen smirked.

"I know," Massie admitted. "But her friends were really
bugging me."

Everyone burst into laughter.

"*Shave* it for someone who cares," Dylan howled, tears
running down her cheeks.

Alicia was laughing so hard, her boobs shook. "Life's an
itch!"

Massie's iPhone *bwoop*ed.

"Is it Claire?" Dylan asked.

Alicia looked over Massie's shoulder. "OMG, it's Landon."

Landon: My birthday is Tues. U and Bean want to
come 4 cake?

"Is 'cake' code for 'lip-kissing'?" Dylan balanced on her
tippy-toes to get a glimpse of Massie's screen.

"Yeah, he just loves lip-kissing Bean," Massie snapped,
feeling slightly unnerved by her crush's offer. It wasn't that
she didn't like Landon. From his blue-green eyes to his rugged
preppyness and his high level of pug appreciation, Massie
had no complaints. But the idea of lip-kissing him threw her
off-kilter. It had been months since she had lip-kissed Derrington. What if she'd forgotten how? What if she got a sudden lip spasm and drooled on Landon? What if techniques had

changed and she'd missed the *Cosmo* article that detailed the updated kiss-dos and -don'ts? Landon was a hawt ninth-grader who was probably at least nine times more experienced than she was. What if she didn't measure up?

"Come awn," Alicia teased. "You know he's gonna want to give you a taste of his *cake*."

The girls giggled. Massie tried to smile.

"What are you going to wear for your first cake?" Kristen asked, spreading a dollop of face mask over her smooth forehead.

"Something by Anna Sui?" said Dylan, waving a frilly red ruffled blouse like a toreador.

Massie wrinkled her nose, hoping her friends thought her look of horror had to do with fashion rather than lip-passion. "Too sweet."

"Prada!" said Alicia.

"Nada," said Massie. "A little *too* sophisticated."

Dylan held up a black sequined top. "Marc always knows what men like."

"Maybe something French?" Alicia tried, slipping into a nude Lacroix heel.

Kristen's green eyes widened. "Ehmagawd. What if Landon wants to kiss you . . . *en français*?"

"In French class?" Dylan asked.

"No, like THIS!" Alicia stuck out her tongue and waggled it around. Kristen exploded into laughter. Dylan made fake smooching sounds. Massie tried her very best not to melt into a puddle of Chanel No. 19–scented sweat.

What if Landon was into extreme lip-kissing? She had seen people do it in movies, and there seemed to be a lot of neck movement involved. But what was actually going on *inside* their mouth? It was like the tapered harem pants trend— totally baffling.

But the alpha couldn't expose her jumpy nerves. Her betas expected her to know everything and to approach life with confidence and knowledge. Instinctively, Massie peeked out at the guesthouse again. Her subconscious guided her toward Claire, just as it always did during times of insecurity. But she was nowhere in sight. Massie would have to deal with this one alone.

Her iPhone *bwoop*ed again.

Landon: Is that a yes?

"Someone's hungry for some cake," Alicia giggled.

"Too bad," Massie declared authoritatively. "*No one's* eating *cake* with all that H1N1 going around. It's unsafe!"

"Puh-lease," Alicia rolled her big brown eyes. "That's so last year."

Dylan took a swig of her Red Bull. "Swiiiiiiiiiiiiiiiiiiiiiiiiiiiiine fluuuuuuuuuuuu," she burped.

Kristen laughed so hard, she snorted like a pig.

"See?" Massie pointed. "Kristen just got it!"

"Whatevs." Alicia petted her faux-rabbit pillowcase. "I'd get the *swine* from someone that *fine*." She grabbed Massie's iPhone.

"Hey!" Massie lunged toward her like she was at a Tory Burch sample sale and Alicia was the last pair of gold-embellished T-strap wedge sandals. "Give that back!"

"I WANT UR LIPS TO LAND ON ME!" Alicia typed, her fingers flying over the keypad. "Get it?" she asked. "LAND-on."

Massie grabbed Alicia's arm, knocking the phone to the floor. She reached for it, but Kristen busted out some crazy soccer move and leg-swept it away. Then, lifting it with her toes, Kristen popped it into her hand.

"Impressive," Dylan marveled.

Kristen smiled her thanks while she typed. "LET'S SWAP SWINE!"

Dylan grabbed the phone. "I've got it: HAVE YOUR CAKE AND EAT IT TOO . . . OFF MY LIPS."

"Hand that over, or I'm going to give you the Todd Cut while you're sleeping!" Massie growled.

Dylan tossed her the phone. Massie caught it in her right hand, her thumb grazing the screen.

Bwoooooop!

Oh no.

No.

No no no no noooo.

The snow outside seemed to stop swirling. Dylan froze mid-laugh. Alicia paused mid-gloss. Kristen's mouth fixed in a round *O*. Bean rolled over and played dead. Massie wished she would die for real.

"Eh-ma-killmenow!" she wailed. "That message just got sent!"

After a quick exchange of nervous glances, the girls snapped into emergency advice mode.

"Maybe he lost his phone," Dylan said quietly.

"Maybe he went blind," Kristen offered.

"Maybe Bark chewed his phone," Alicia tried.

"Yeah," Dylan added. "Like an iBone."

"Opposite of funny!" Massie wailed.

Just then she heard the tune from "You Belong with Me"— Landon's exclusive ringtone.

Landon: ☺ U read my mind. ☺

"Ehmagawd," Massie gasped. "He thinks I sent those! Now what?"

Alicia tossed Massie her dented tube of Clarins lip balm. "Start moisturizing, that's what."

A yogurt-cover pretzel began inching its way back up Massie's throat. It was obviously freaking out, too, and eager to escape. If only it could take her with it.

Claire grinned and tugged on the tassels of her new blue hat. Life was good.

When she'd first learned of Massie's Friday-night sleepovers, she'd envisioned late nights full of bedazzling, crafting friendship bracelets and gum-wrapper chains, *Gilmore Girls* marathons, and pajama dance parties. And then she'd actually attended one and her vision was scared away, leaving behind a dust cloud of shattered dreams and an overnight bag filled with unstrung beads and fishing wire.

But now, after a yearlong absence, those sleepover visions had finally returned. Only this time, they were real. And even better than she had imagined.

Claire and her mom had transformed their cozy living room into a veritable Candy Land. Overflowing bowls of marshmallows, graham crackers, Hershey's chocolate bars, gummy feet, and jelly beans tempted her guests to indulge their sweet teeth and fatten their funny bones. Sugar substitutes and the dreaded *f*-words—"fat" and "free"—were not invited.

"Beep . . . beep . . . beep," Layne said, impersonating a truck while she backed a triple-decker s'more into her mouth. Her nostrils flared as she attempted to chew the wide load. Claire gagged a little as Layne's green eyes began to water.

"Ahhhhh." Layne finally swallowed. "Those remind me of Girl Scouts."

"You were a Girl Scout?" Cara asked while sideswiping her bangs.

"No." Layne lay back on the sage-colored carpet and rubbed her protruding belly. "I'm talking about the cookies. If they gave out badges for eating those things, I'd look like a patchwork quilt."

"You're going to look like a duvet if you don't ease up," Claire joked.

Layne lifted her head and shot her friend a pained glance. It stung like a slap on the cheek.

Claire quickly apologized. Not so much because she'd insulted Layne, but because her comment had sounded judgmental and controlling. In fact, it bordered on fat-phobic. It was a Massie comment. Like a cough that lingers after the cold is gone, Claire still had traces of the alpha in her system. For that she truly was truly sorry, and she popped two marshmallows in her mouth to prove it.

Layne showed her that all was forgiven with a soft smile and the renewed desire to decorate her toenails with mini rhinestones.

Syd sat cross-legged at the wooden coffee table, sewing soda-can tabs onto a sustainable metallic clutch, the tip of her tongue sticking out between her gold-glossed lips. Cara was making an eco-friendly makeup brush holder out of recycled Popsicle sticks.

"Do you think I should make a separate one for eyeliner or just put them all in the same holder?" Cara asked.

"What leaves a smaller carbon footprint?" Syd replied, with a sewing needle between her lips.

"Smaller carbon feet," Layne offered.

The girls burst out laughing.

"Like these?" Claire wiggled her toes inside her fuzzy, googley-eyed frog socks, and the girls laughed even harder.

Massie would have thought Layne's joke was lame times ten—and that Claire's socks were an insult to amphibians. But Claire quickly reminded herself that Massie's opinions no longer mattered. Sure, the hat was a nice gesture. But it wasn't enough to make Claire turn against her new friends. Nothing was—or would ever be again.

"Hey, Syd," Layne said, waving her rhinestones dry. "Do ninth-grade boys like independent women?"

Syd pushed her clutch aside and contemplated the question. She obviously took great pride in being the only girl at the sleepover with a high school boyfriend. And she clearly wanted to give her impressionable students sound advice. "I think it depends on the guy." She sat up on her knees and folded her hands on the coffee table. "Like Doug, for example. He's glad I have plans with you guys tonight, but that's only because he doesn't have band practice. If he had practice, he'd definitely want me there." She glanced at the home screen on her phone. It was a picture of Doug and his reggae band, Smells Like Uncle Hugh, standing in front of a Bob Marley poster at Spencer Gifts. "So I guess it's all about balance and communication."

Cara nodded in agreement.

"So which musicians make the best boyfriends?" Claire asked.

The girls looked at her with devilish curiosity.

"No," Claire giggled nervously. "It's not like that. I was just wondering. I swear. Cam and I are great." Her cheeks burned.

"Well"—Syd leaned forward on her elbows—"if you're ever looking for an upgrade, I'd say go for the drummer."

They asked her why.

"He's all the way in the back," she explained. "He gets no attention whatsoever, so his ego is typically smaller—"

"And you know what they say about drummers with small egos," Cara snickered.

Layne and Claire exchanged confused glances.

"Big sticks!" the ninth graders shouted together.

Layne, her feet stretched out in front of her, speed-scooted her butt closer to the coffee table. "What else?"

"Dictation!" Syd insisted.

Claire and Layne cracked the spines of their newly purchased recycled notebooks, their matching scented glow-in-the-dark candy cane pens hovering above the wood-flecked paper. They were ready for their daily dose of high school wisdom.

"Syd and Cara's Guy-dlines," Syd announced.

Claire copied down the title and underlined it twice.

"Number one," Cara began. "Guys who listen, we'll be kissin'."

"If his style is lame, he's got no game," Syd continued.

One by one, the girls took turns reciting their Guy-dlines while Claire and Layne wrote at a fat-burning pace.

If he uses too much mousse, cut him loose.

If he's mean, he's off the scene.

If he's a flirt, make him hurt.

If he loves your pet, you're all set.

If he calls you fat, block him on G-chat.

If he has BO, the answer is **no.**

If he doesn't own soap, the answer is **nope.**

If bikini babes are on his walls, screen his calls.

If he makes good jokes, return his Facebook pokes.

Acting like a mute is **so** not cute.

If he won't admit to crying, he's heartless or lying!

T-zone too slick? Make a new pick.

If he ignores you at school, the guy's a fool.

If he burps in your face, you must replace.

If your photos cover the inside of his locker, he's a stalker.

If he has an earring, consider disappearing!

If he can't score a goal, stop, drop, and roll.

If he won't return a text, move on to the next.

If he's rude to your mother, go find another.

Rude to your pop? Close up shop.

If he's a bad kisser, find your inner disser.

If he fails driver's ed, date his friend instead.

If you catch him in a lie, find an honest guy.

If he has no muscle, time to hustle.

If he doesn't think you're funny, the boy ain't money.

If he'd rather play Wii, *hasta la vista, baybeeeeeee.*

"I have one," Claire said. "If his eyes don't match, he's a good catch."

"Nice," Cara applauded.

"How about . . ." Layne waggled her unplucked brows. "Use a brush, or no crush."

"No floss, his loss," Syd giggled.

Claire scribbled furiously.

Bzzzzzzzzz.

The oven timer interrupted their list making.

"Cookies are ready!" Claire tossed her notebook on the coffee table and hurried to the kitchen. Her mom was standing over the wooden butcher's block, flipping through the paper, her brown bun held in place by a meat thermometer.

Judi Lyons pushed her reading glasses onto her forehead. "Having fun?"

Claire smiled. "Yeah. Lots."

"I can tell. You're acting like my little Claire Bear again." She pulled her daughter in for a hug.

"Moooooooooooom." Claire wiggled out of her mom's grasp.

"Sorry. Was I acting like an LBR?"

"Stop," Claire shuddered at her mother's attempt to speak Massie.

"*What?*" Judi bit her bottom lip. "Does that make you miss her?"

"No," Claire insisted. "It makes me miss *you.*"

Mrs. Lyons laughed, and then slid the red-and-white-gingham oven mitts toward her daughter.

Claire lifted the holiday-scented cinnamon cookies out of the oven and arranged them on a pink heart-shaped serving tray. Her mother was right. She was feeling like her old self again. No one had criticized her clothing, called her *Kuh-laire,* or questioned her about her friends in weeks. It was more liberating than a skinny-dip in August.

"Did someone order Cinnabon?" Claire bellowed, returning to her friends with a tray full of chewy love.

The girls didn't respond. They didn't even look at her. They were squat-huddled over Layne's iPhone, distracted by something major. By the look of their intensity, it seemed like more drama than a mere 3G device could deliver.

Claire set the cookies down on the fireplace mantel and hurried over.

"No wayyyyy," Cara said. "I'm not shaving my head!"

Syd pulled anxiously on her short brown bob. "That look didn't work for Natalie Portman in *Vendetta,* and it won't work for me."

Claire knelt down next to Layne. "What's going on?"

Syd shot back three feet and cowered next to the fire. Cara clutched a Popsicle stick so tight, it broke in half.

"Nothing." Layne tried to hide the phone behind her back, but Claire snatched it out of her hands.

Massie: Heads up! There's a louse in the house. Y do U think Todd shaved his head? Make sure Claire doesn't wear Todd's blue hat. Sleep tight. Don't let the head bugs bite! ΛOΛ

Claire whipped off the hat.

"Ehh!" Syd gasped, scrambling to her feet. "Don't spray them!"

Cara grabbed her tie-dyed canvas bag and quickly covered her head.

The gummies in Claire's stomach joined together for a group hug in a gooey show of support. "I don't have lice," she cried in a mass of anger and desperation. "And neither does Todd!"

"Then why would May-see say you did?" Cara challenged.

Syd put her hands on her hips. "Yeah, and why would your brother shave his head? It's obviously not flattering, so . . ."

"Because she's Mah-ssie," Claire explained. "She's mad that I'm hanging out with you, and she's trying to scare you away."

"That's quite an elaborate plan, wouldn't you say?" Syd said, stuffing her pop-top clutch with the sewing supplies.

"Not for her," Layne said, sounding unimpressed by the alpha's latest scheme. But she was obviously trying to comfort Claire, because even *she* had to admit it was an impressive—albeit demented, self-centered, and malicious—scheme.

Cara rubbed the duffel against her scalp, tending to an itch that wasn't there. "That's a lot of trouble to go through just to get back at someone."

"Here's a rule," Syd added, grabbing Cara by the wrist. "If there's lice in the hair, get outta there!"

Cara nodded, allowing herself to be pulled toward the front door.

"I need a Brillo-bath—stat," Syd said, with a squirmy wiggle.

"Wait! I promise, no one has lice!" Claire cried.

But her words fell on panic-stricken ears, and faster than she could say, "RID," her new friends took off.

Hot tears prickled at the back of Claire's eyes. She felt a heavy arm plop down over her shoulders. "You're not leaving too, are you?" she asked Layne, her voice shaking.

"No to the way," Layne said. A smile spread over her lips. "I had lice once, and I happen to love the shampoo. It smells like science camp."

Claire hung her head. "I don't have lice."

"I know," Layne said simply. "If they believe you have lice, they aren't very nice."

Claire linked her arm through Layne's. "A friend that is true, will stand by you," she would have said if she thought she could speak without crying. Instead, she tried to inhale the comforting smell of cinnamon cookies.

But that, too, was gone.

"Kiwi Strawberry?" suggested Dylan.

Massie shook her head. "Landon once told me kiwis make his lips itch."

"Well, then you could scratch his lips with yours!"

"Eww!" Alicia tossed a fuzzy slipper at Dylan's head.

"Candy Cane?" Kristen called out.

"Then he'll think she's trying to cover up bad breath." Alicia turned toward Massie. "I mean, not that you would be."

"Cayenne Pepper?" Dylan asked.

"Too hawt to handle!" Massie joked.

Kristen squinted at a green tube. "This looks like mold."

"Toss it," Massie instructed. "I never liked the Caesar Salad flavor."

"Okay, what about Passion Fruit!"

"Or Vanilla Bliss."

"Vanilla *KISS*!"

"Ha ha," Massie said drily.

She'd awoken that morning with a smile on her face. Two sets of fresh footsteps had led away from the guesthouse, meaning she'd successfully defriended Claire the previous night. But then she'd received a text from Landon, reminding her that it was T-minus three days until their first lip kiss, and her heart had plummeted faster than Tiger Woods's career. Now she and her friends were standing in front of Gloss Row, a glass-encased wall of her closet that contained her entire lip gloss collection, trying to decide which gloss would be most effective for kissing an older man.

Alicia pushed her dark hair off her shoulder. "We should play gloss tarot to see what the kiss will be like."

"What's that?" Dylan asked.

"Massie closes her eyes and picks a gloss from her collection," Alicia answered. "Then whatever flavor it is, it'll tell her something about what the kiss will be like."

Massie rolled her eyes, but Kristen and Dylan nodded eagerly.

"Where'd you learn that?" Dylan asked.

"My cousin Nina went to this psychic last weekend who said that if you have a question and you concentrate on channeling the energy of the question out into the universe, you can tell your fortune with almost anything." Alicia shrugged.

Massie was about to make a crack about Alicia's cousin's brain being out of the universe, but a wave of kiss-anxiety hit her, so she closed her eyes and plucked one of the glosses from the pile.

"MASSIE!"

Massie's eyes flew open as Claire burst into her bedroom. She wore ripped, straight-leg jeans and a blue-and-yellow striped waffle tee under a fleece vest. She looked ready for a day of hiking—or arguing over the bargain bin at T.J. Maxx. "I. DON'T. HAVE. LICE."

Massie smirked. "I never said you did. I just asked *Layme* why she thought Todd had to have his head shaved."

"All my friends left because of you!" Claire put her hands on her hips. "You were trying to ruin my party."

"Puh-lease." Massie rolled her eyes. "The only thing that ruined your sleepover was frizzy hair and bad music."

Massie and Claire glared at each other, while Alicia, Dylan, and Kristen exchanged nervous glances. The tension was as thick and goopy as expired nail polish.

"Well," Massie said finally, "I hate to add *insect* to injury, but do you know what *this* sleepover has in common with the Oscars?"

Claire didn't speak or move a muscle. She stood there, arms crossed, unblinking.

"What?" Dylan said finally, clearly trying to release the tension.

"It's only for the A-list!"

With that, Claire turned and stormed out, slamming the door behind her.

"Wow." Dylan breathed. "She was totally *bugged* out."

"I take my hat off to you, Massie." Alicia fake-curtsied.

While the Pretty Committee continued to joke, Massie rested her forehead on her window. Outside, Claire was stomping her way back across the snow-covered lawn. The Pretty Committee continued to joke, and Massie knew she should feel triumphant. She had bombed Claire's sleepover into oblivion with one fake lice-infested snow hat. But as Claire kicked the snow-Cam, Massie's pride melted into something more akin to regret.

Sure, Claire didn't know anything about footwear or fashion. She had no idea how to pick a deep conditioner or a facial scrub. But unlike the rest of the PC, she was an experienced lip-kisser with nearly a year of practice, and she would never judge Massie for being nervous about kissing an older guy. Had Massie just alienated her only hope for helpful lip-to-lip tips?

"Hey, Mass," Alicia said. "What flavor of gloss did you pick?"

Massie snapped back into focus. She looked down at the gloss in her hand. When she saw the writing on the tube, her cheeks flamed like a bonfire doused in lighter fluid.

"Spaghetti Bolognese," she mumbled. Laughter filled the room.

Massie bit her lip and didn't even bother to try to laugh along with her friends. Because if she didn't manage to figure out how to kiss like a ninth-grader—and soon—she'd be dead meat.

CURRENT STATE OF THE UNION	
IN	**OUT**
Hair scare	Hair care
Old enemies	New friends
Dissing lice	Kissing advice

Saturday afternoon, Claire crossed the threshold of Sweet-sations Candy Shoppe, with Cam and Layne at each waffle-shirt-clad elbow. Immediately the scent of sugar coated her every pore, buoying her spirits like a surfboard in the waves.

"Better?" Cam nudge-asked her.

"Much," Claire answer-nudged back. When Cam had stopped by her house that morning to drop off a new mix CD before soccer practice, she'd felt sadder than the last LBR to be picked in gym class. She and Layne had been brainstorming revenge plots against Massie, but they kept coming up empty-handed. Cam had taken one look at Claire's face and announced he was taking her and Layne to Sweetsations, a new buffet-style sweet shop where they could get all-you-can-eat candy for $14.99 a pound.

"For you." Cam handed Layne and Claire each a wooden tray, and they got in line behind a seven-year-old with jelly stains down his back.

The shop was packed fuller than Six Flags on opening day. Kori and Strawberry, two girls from OCD, were crowded around a dark-chocolate dipping fountain, fonduing candy canes and apple slices. Twin pigtailed girls grabbed umbrella-shaped lollipops and edible rings as their parents looked on. A five-year-old boy licked the blueberry rock-candy wall at the back of the store while his older sister measured out a yard of sugar dots. A couple of sixth-grade boys *ooh*ed and *ahh*ed at a collection of chocolate-covered insects near the counter. One girl in a Hannah Montana T-shirt bent over a standard-issue trash bin and tossed her cookies. Literally.

"Ew," Claire and Cam said at the same time.

"Jinx." Cam crush-punched Claire on the shoulder. Love waves radiated from her arm to her heart.

"How much do you think it would cost to buy this place?" Layne said, popping a caramel into her mouth. Her giraffe-print galoshes squeegeed against the black-and-white marble floor, leaving a trail of slush in her wake.

Cam held up a fistful of foiled gold coins. "One *mill-yon* coins," he said in a dead-on Dr. Evil impersonation. Claire grinned. With little blond tufts sticking out of his Billabong hat, Cam looked cute times ten.

"Clar, aht do oo tink?" Layne said in a muffled voice. She wore a set of giant wax candy lips. "The lip implant went really well, no?"

Claire laughed. "Absolutely."

"Hey." Cam touched Claire's hand. "Isn't that your brother?"

Claire scanned the store for Todd; it was a 3-D Where's Baldo? moment. A couple of kids ran figure eights through the picnic-style tables in the back, while others applied chocolate pudding like face paint. Her eyes snagged on the Jelly Beanery section, where a shiny head reflected the store's fluorescent light like polished silver.

And just like that, Claire's good mood tarnished. She motioned for her friends to follow her.

". . . five of each color should do it?" Tiny Nathan was asking as Claire, Layne, and Cam came up behind them.

"Maybe six of the green ones would be better?" Todd said, holding a green bean up to the light like he was inspecting a diamond for flaws.

"Echem," Claire coughed.

Todd whirled around and hid the bag of beans behind his back. "Yo. What up?"

"What up?" Layne sucked on the giant wax lips like they were a pacifier.

"Looking slick, dudes." Cam nod-flicked his blond bangs out of his blue eye.

"You know it." Todd sucked in his cheeks while Tiny Nathan crossed his arms over his hoodie.

Claire dug her nails into her palms to stop herself from laughing out loud. "So. I have a proposition for you."

Todd raised a red brow. "I'm listening."

Someone jostled Claire from behind, knocking her into her brother. Oddly, the little freak smelled like Old Spice. She regained her balance and took a step back. "You, me, whoever else, need to get revenge on Massie for shaving your head."

"Sorry, sister. No can do." Todd shook his head.

Layne took her lips off and gnawed on the cherry-flavored wax. One of the sixth-grade boys stared at her, then nudged his friends and ran to get his own set.

Claire stared at him in disbelief. "What? Why? She made you *bald*."

"Noooo," Todd said slowly, nodding. "She gave me a new lease on life."

"The man looked so good, I went and got the same 'do myself!" Tiny Nathan added, pulling off his hat. Red, irritated splotches bloomed across his bumpy skull like a Rorschach pattern.

Claire tapped her booted foot. They just weren't getting it. "She gave you razor burn so my new friends would think you had lice and ditch me."

Todd blinked and shook his head, like he couldn't believe how naïve Claire was being. "Look," he said, throwing back his shoulders. "I can't imagine why Massie would make me this hot and then set me free to meet other chicks. But over seven girls have checked me out in the last ten minutes, and Sarah Derkins told me I look *bad*!" Todd chin-nodded at a girl in the fudge section.

"She was right," Layne mumbled.

Claire giggled into her palm.

Todd ran his hands over his scalp. "Plus, the five o'clock shadow makes me look at least twelve."

Tiny Nathan rolled back on his blue Simples, looking tinier than ever in his oversized clothes. "At least."

Todd flexed his biceps, then pulled six Pixy Stix from his back pocket. He handed three to Nathan. "Bottoms up!" he said. He and Nathan tilted their heads back and shot them down all at the same time.

"Yup, that's the stuff!" Tiny Nathan squeaked.

Just then, a group of girls ambled by, whispering and giggling and pointing. "See?" Todd said, triumphantly. "Now if you'll excuse me . . ." With that, he twisted the tie on his bag of jelly beans and sauntered over to the counter, where he proceeded to tap a redhead on the shoulder. When she turned around, he grabbed a handful of chocolate covered ants and shoved them in his mouth.

"Ahhhhh!" the girl screamed, and she ran out of the store while Tiny Nathan cheered and high-fived Todd.

"I don't know what just happened, but my head hurts," Layne said, massaging her temples with one hand. With the other she rolled the mashed-up wax into a tube.

"Maybe you're waxtose intolerant," Cam suggested.

Claire stood and watched Todd and Tiny Nathan high-five their way out of the store. "I can't believe he said no." Todd *never* turned down a chance to scheme. It was like Claire, Cam, and Layne were the only people immune to Massie's evil charms.

"Sorry." Cam comfort-punched Claire in the shoulder. He handed her a paper bag filled with lemon drops. She unwrapped the candy and slipped it between her cherry Chapsticked lips. As the first tangy pellet hit her tongue, Claire remembered how lucky she was to have someone like Cam, who gave her sweets when she was feeling like a Sour Patch Kid. "But maybe it's better this way," he suggested. "Maybe you don't need to get revenge after all."

"Well, maybe she doesn't *need* to," Layne said, taking a

lemon drop. "And maybe I don't *need* to buy six more sets of these wax lips. But I'm going to." She pointed to her wrist, around which was affixed a cherry-scented red wax bracelet, shiny with spit. "Anyway, you don't need Todd for our revenge plot. I'll help you."

Claire's lips puckered as the lemon candy melted in her mouth. It almost hurt to eat it, but she always felt like she'd accomplished something when she made it down to the sweet part. She bit into the lemon drop, forcing herself to chew through the pain. And by the time the candy was gone, she knew it was time to move onto the sweetest part of her day.

The revenge.

Massie leaned back against her 3,000-thread-count silk sheets and kicked the fully clothed Massiequin with one of her BCBG riding boots. "I don't know, Bean," she said to the puppy, who was curled in her lap. "Is it missing something?"

The Massiequin was adorned in her latest attempt at a kiss outfit: a Rag & Bone silk-trimmed cropped vest over a long aquamarine Yaya Aflalo tank and a pair of dark denim skinny jeans. On the floor next to it was her earlier choice: a blue-green Marc Jacobs silk dress, which she'd since vetoed. Sure, it looked hawt on her, and the color would match Landon's eyes, but it reeked of "special occasion," and the last thing she wanted was for Landon to think their first kiss was a moment she'd dressed up for.

With only two days left until Landon's birthday, Massie was having major kiss-ues. Sure, he'd sent her Twitter pics of him and Bark playing in the snow, and even one where he'd carved BOC + BB within the outline of a dog in the snow. But Landon's ah-dorableness only set her teeth more on edge.

What was wrong with her? She was Massie Block, alpha of the Pretty Committee. She'd lip-kissed Derrington, of course. So why was she nervous? Was it because Landon was older? Because she liked him times ten? Was it because, as the alpha, there was simply more pressure on her to be perfect? People like Layne and Claire had no idea how easy they had it. No one would expect their kisses to be perfect 10s. But Massie's had to be off the chart.

There was only one place to turn: her anti-anxiety audiobook. Opening iTunes, she clicked on "Part 1" of *Declouding Your Inner Self: A Guide to Overcoming Anxiety*.

A woman's deep voice flowed out of the Bose speakers. "WELCOME TO THE NEW, MORE RELAXED YOU."

Massie skipped right to the mantra tracks.

"IMAGINE YOU ARE BEING FILLED WITH A CALM BLUE LIGHT."

She lay back on her comforter, letting it envelop her like a downy crepe, and closed her eyes.

"THIS CALM BLUE LIGHT IS VERY CALM AND VERY BLUE."

She imagined the blue light was the color of Landon's eyes.

"THIS CALM BLUE LIGHT IS WORKING ITS WAY THROUGH YOUR HEART AND YOUR SACRUM AND FLOWING DOWN YOUR LEGS AND ARMS. NOW PICTURE A FLUFFY CLOUD . . ."

Massie pictured a cotton ball in the shape of Landon's head, complete with his Adrian Grenier–esque tousled curls.

"FLUFFIER," instructed the voice.

With her mind's eye, Massie fluffed up Landon's cloud hair a fraction of an inch.

"EVEN FLUFFIER!"

"I'm trying!" Massie whined, opening her eyes for a split second to glare at the speakers.

"GOOD," the voice said. "NOW GATHER YOUR WORST FEARS, AND PLACE THEM ONE BY ONE ON THE FLUFFY CLOUD."

Closing her eyes again, Massie took her fear of lip-kissing an older man, her fear that the PC would abandon her, her fear that shoulder pads might make a comeback, and she placed them one by one on the Landon cloud.

Then the woman's voice instructed, "NOW BLOW THE CLOUD AWAY."

Massie inhaled deeply, then blew as hard as she could. The cloud shuddered but stayed put.

"Go away," Massie blew again. Nothing.

"BLOW THE CLOUD FAR, FAR AWAY," the woman's voice barked.

Massie tried to push the cloud away, but it was as fruitless as trying to fit her size 6 foot into a size 5 wedge. The cloud was enormous—larger than the entire Block Estate—and the harder she blew, the more twisted her fears looked. Landon's lips parted into a sinister grin. Fear-replicas of Kristen, Dylan, and Alicia pointed and laughed at her. And gigantic, powder-pink shoulder pads zoomed toward her, threatening to suffocate her where she stood.

"PUSH!" The woman boomed.

"GO AWAY!" Massie yelled at her fears.

Bean whimpered and jumped off the bed.

Massie opened one eye. "Not you, Bean. The fear cloud!"

But it was useless. And now she had another fear to add to the pile: a fear of massive, immovable clouds.

Sighing, she shut off the audiobook and clicked onto Firefox. First she googled "kissing techniques," but when that delivered a series of blocked sites, she decided to get specific. Within minutes, she had compiled a list of the hawtest, most important lip kisses of all time:

- THE MYS KISS, *Spider-Man* (2003), Kirsten Dunst and Tobey McGuire: Mys-terious Spidey is hanging upside down. She pulls off half his mask and kisses him.

- THE RISK KISS, *Twilight* (2008), Kristen Stewart and Robert Pattinson: She risks her life to kiss a vampire.

- THE DISS KISS, MTV Video Music Awards (2009), Kristen Stewart and Robert Pattinson (again): Accepting their award for Best Kiss, Robert ditches his gum and everything, but at the last minute, Kristen pulls away. (Okay, technically not a kiss—but they totally kissed off-camera later!)

- THE AQUA-BLISS KISS, *The Notebook* (2005), Rachel McAdams and Ryan Gosling: Kissing in the rain.

- THE HISS KISS, *Gossip Girl* (Season Two): Serena kisses Nate at a party to make his cougar girlfriend jealous. Meow!

Massie closed her laptop. Okay, so Landon was easily as hawt as a superhero, but it seemed unlikely that he'd be hanging upside down during their smooch. And since she wasn't famous (yet), she probably wasn't going to win an MTV Video Music Award. It was possible they could kiss in the rain like Rachel McAdams and Ryan Gosling, but that would mean ruining her blowout and risking raccoon eyes.

No, none of those kisses felt exactly right. Maybe if she took the mystery of the Mys Kiss, added the danger of the Risk Kiss, the longing of the Diss Kiss, the passion of the Aqua-Bliss Kiss, and the confidence of the Hiss Kiss, she would get what she was hoping for—the Mass Kiss.

Taking a breath, she shut her blinds and replaced her anti-stress CD with *Sounds of the Brazilian Rain Forest,* uncapped her Passion Fruit Glossip Girl, put Landon's sweatshirt on the Massiequin, and paw-swore Bean to secrecy. She closed her eyes, praying her life would never get more pathetic than it was at that particular moment.

And then she puckered up for practice.

In times of crisis, Claire usually sought out sugar. Mike and Ike had gotten her through the road trip from Orlando to Westchester. Reese's Pieces were the official sponsor of her short-lived Cam breakup. And gummies had eased the stress of life in the public eye as a (former) member of the PC. But as she and Layne stepped out of the snowy Westchester tundra and entered the humid mock-jungle of Karma Chameleon, she knew her current situation required more than a Blow Pop.

It required bugs.

Claire stomped the excess snow from her Keds onto the peeling linoleum floor and looked around. The store smelled like a mixture of the bottom of Todd's sock drawer and old, crusty peanut butter. Glass aquariums filled with mossy water were stacked everywhere, and she had the uneasy feeling that thousands of moist, shifty eyeballs were watching her every move. Posters papered the steamy walls like a who's who of creepy crawlers. A lizard in a Santa hat with a leering expression yelled, ALL I IGUANA FOR CHRISTMAS IS YOU. Next to it was a cobra wearing a New York Yankees hat with SNAKE ME OUT TO THE BALLGAME printed under it. And next to that was a gecko sitting on a waffle that had popped out of a toaster.

"Gecko my Eggo." Layne's laugh came from behind the

netting of her boxy white beekeeper hat. "Ooooh! Wook how kuh-ute!" She pulled Claire past a row of oversize snakes to a python tank the size of the Lyons' old minivan. As Layne cooed and tapped the aquarium, one of the python's olive-black eyes blinked lazily. Then its tongue shot out of its mouth to snatch an unsuspecting beetle. Claire thought of her lunch that day and wondered if she was about to see it again.

"Mwah!" Layne blew the python a kiss. "I IGUANA him for my very own."

"Um, Layne." Claire pointed to a sign affixed to the habitat. A neon sticky said: I'M CANDY! I LIKE TO BE FED CRICKETS AND MICE.

"Deal breaker." Layne spun in a circle, her coattails floating out around her like a tutu. She grinned. "Maybe I should take that one home instead?"

Claire followed the direction in which her friend's gnawed fingernail was pointing, but instead of finding a reptile, she saw a lanky boy wearing a faded Phoenix T-shirt and a pair of dark-wash denim skinnys.

"Layne," Claire whispered, the moldy scent of brackish water clogging her nostrils. "He's in violation of rule number 21. I think that grasshopper weighs more than he does."

"It's unlawful to discriminate based on age or weight," said Layne, beelining toward the boy like a hawt-seeking missile.

"Hi, there," he said when they reached the counter. His name tag read ART, and up close it was impossible to miss just how much his dark, round eyes resembled Candy's. Claire shuddered.

Layne curled her oversize foot around her left leg, then tilted her head in her patented cute-boy shuffle. The beekeeper hat shifted back, and she lost her balance. Claire grabbed her friend's shoulder to steady her.

"I love your hat," Art said. "It's for bees, right?"

Layne adjusted the netting like a traditional bride trying to conceal herself. "None of your *beeswax*." She giggled.

Art grinned. "So what can I help you with?"

Layne leaned her elbows on the distressed wooden counter. Clustered around the register were pink bottles of Natural Chemistry Healthy Habitat spray, Tetrafauna Baby ReptoMin food sticks, and bags of shredded wood bedding. "We're having trouble deciding. But we don't want to *bug* you."

"No problem." He blinked quickly, still looking remarkably like the shifty python they'd just encountered. "My mother always *toad* me to be kind to strangers."

Claire rolled back on her heels, the way she always did when she was annoyed and anxious. "We just want some smaller bugs," she said, hoping her brisk tone would help move things along. "Like, some bedbugs." *To go in a certain alpha's bed,* she added silently.

"I know just the thing!" Art said. He slunk around the counter, then loped down an aisle of bright yellow saltwater fish. Layne's eyes followed him, and she licked her half-eaten wax lips. She'd been feasting on them since they had left the candy store—their second visit that week—and they looked half digested.

Claire elbowed Layne through her puffy coat. "Don't forget the mission," she hissed.

Layne ignored her, following close behind Art's doodled-on yellow Converse as he led them past a wall of turtles, then through a dark room with tanks lining the walls. One tank let out a long hiss. It sounded like *I know what you're doing!* A second later, a bunch of frogs in a grimy aquarium chimed in with a chorus of *Mean! Mean! Mean!*

"She deserves it!" Claire hissed back. "What would you do if someone scared off all your friends?" The frogs blinked back at her and tilted their heads.

Normally, Claire wasn't the type to hold a grudge. Everyone made mistakes sometimes—she knew that. But when she looked back over her year and three months of "friendship" with Massie, it was all the bad times that stuck out. Counting the list of Massie-caused grievances was easier than making slice and bake cookies. She started ticking them off on her fingers.

She insulted the friendship bracelets my friends in Orlando made me, by pretending to think they were from kindergarten.

She left me in the trunk of the Range Rover on the first day of seventh grade.

She told me OCD stood for *Orlando Claire = Dork*.

She asked me if I was invited to her barbecue, and

then when I said no, she asked me why I was up in her grill. This was the first of many, many, many, many, MANY similar insults. Too many to list. Just know: IT STARTED HERE.

She put red paint on my pants so it looked like I got my period. (Okay, Alicia actually did that, but she wouldn't have done it if Massie hadn't decided she hated me.)

She kicked me out of their first sleepover (practically, by being mean).

She said my brown sweatshirt looked like a hooded poo.

She said my pink belt made me looked like a pink boa constrictor had wrapped itself around my face and then died from shock at how bad my outfit was.

She threw *salmon* at me!

She told everyone that our joint Halloween party was just *her* party.

She said my geeky-loser costume was very convincing and asked if I was celebrating Halloween early that year.

She said my green apple gummies looked like alien sneeze.

She told me that just because matchy-matchy wasn't in, it did nawt mean clashy-clashy was.

She called me stupid for not knowing that some dressing rooms use super-flattering skinny mirrors.

She threw out my favorite pants on Earth Day as part of the Beautify Our Planet campaign.

She told me my favorite sweater was making Bean sick because Bean was allergic to ugly.

She said she would've tossed my red sweatshirt in the fire, but she didn't want to release toxic fumes when the synthetic fabric and puffy-paint melted.

She asked if I was getting extra credit in Abnormal Psychology for being friends with Layne.

She said my legs looked like they had Candy Cane Disease when I tried on a pair of striped tights.

She planted Oxy, Jolene face bleach, Depends undergarments, Rogaine, dandruff shampoo, athlete's foot medicine, jock itch cream, and super-plus-sized tampons in the garbage in my trailer on the set of *Dial L for Loser*—and then videotaped a segment about it for *The Daily Grind* to try and convince everyone I had zits, a mustache, bladder control issues, female baldness, dandruff, athlete's foot, jock itch, and a giant period!

She sent Cam a picture of me kissing Connor Foley on the set of *Dial L for Loser* to make him think I was cheating on him. (Which I wasn't!)

She kicked me out of the Pretty Committee. At least eight times.

She wouldn't speak to me for an entire week when I accidentally thought Bean was a French bulldog instead of a pug.

She wouldn't speak to me for two hours when I mentioned that her nut "allergy" only comes out when she doesn't want to eat something.

She wouldn't speak to me for three days when I decided to hang out with Cam instead of watch *Gossip Girl* with her.

She replaced my bag of licorice whips with red rubber bands.

She called my eyebrows the "Bush twins" when I had to wear fake brows for *Dial L*.

She said my bangs looked like the top of my head was throwing up hair.

She called me Clarence when I wore work boots outside to help my mom garden. (There is no such thing as cute, girly gardening shoes!)

She recommended that I see a plastic surgeon because my right ear lobe is a little bigger than my left one.

She recommended that I walk around with weights

on my legs to prevent cankles, because she thinks my mom has them.

She cut up my very favorite BDG hoodie because she ran out of plastic baggies and needed something to pick up Bean's poo with.

She threw out an entire stash of gummy lobsters when she decided she was allergic to shellfish.

She insulted my overalls, even though she complimented the ones that Dylan wore.

She made fun of my mom's mom-jeans. But what else is she supposed to wear? She's a mom!

She locked me out of my own room when I didn't vote for her in the Miss Kiss pageant.

She hit me with a remote control when she thought I was flirting with Dempsey (her then-crush) while on the boy fast.

She tried to force me to upgrade Cam with a new ninth-grade crush. She thought having a crush on a guy with an asymmetric haircut and a crush on a guy with one blue eye and one green eye would be the same thing. As if!

She got mad at me for having ninth-grade friends, even though she'd been telling me that I needed to grow up!

She shaved my little brother's head to get back at me.

She tried to make my new friends think I had a lice infestation.

Claire shook her head at the length of the list. And those were just the highlights. Massie had smacked down Claire more times than her AmEx. Claire pulled a gummy worm from her pocket and popped it in her mouth. The sugar calmed her stomach and reignited her hunger for revenge. Massie had bug-bombed Claire's friends out of her life; it seemed only fitting that Claire would bug-bomb Massie's bed in return.

Art finally stopped in a room with a sign that said ARTHRO-PODOGIE.

"These are your best bet," he said, gesturing to an aquarium with a sandy bottom. A log ran through the center, surrounded by a smattering of rocks and pinecones. Multi-legged creatures with antennae and exoskeletons scurried around the tank. A cricket stood on a twig like a general at arms, while four ants carted a fallen comrade back to their anthill.

"Ew. Those are worse than ugly," cracked Layne. "They're BUG-ly."

"We'll take two of each," Claire said. "Two crickets, two beetles, two centipedes, and two of those pincer-looking things."

Art pushed up a sleeve, showing off a tattoo of a tree frog on the inside of his forearm, and produced a small plastic box from behind the shelf. Inside, he placed a few sticks, a tiny patch of grass, and some dirt he scooped from an empty aquarium nearby.

With a green mesh net, he scooped the requested creepy crawlies into the box. When he was finished, he clamped the habitat shut and handed it to Claire. The bugs crawled all over one another, scratching at the walls like they were trying to get out.

"These latches are secure, right?" she said warily, staring at the box. She handed it to Layne.

They followed the lanky insect lover back to the front of the store, where a pin-thin man in a Sherlock Holmes hat had just entered. Art looked at him over his shoulder. "Be right there, Mr. Harbinger."

Layne cleared her throat. "You know, I should probably get your card. In case I need advice on insect care or, like, a new job."

"Oh, sure." Art quickly scribbled down his name. "Facebook me. Karma Chameleon could always use more help."

Layne beamed. "Well, I guess we'll geck-o-ing."

"Enjoy your new pets!" he called out as the girls walked away.

"Oh, don't worry," Layne giggled, high-fiving Claire. "We will!"

"I still don't understand why no one told *me* about the extra credit," Kristen said, shaking her head as she and Massie entered Auditorium 7 at the Clearview Multiplex. *Liaisons Diaboliques*, a black-and-white French film about a teenage girl who falls desperately in love with a much older vampire, was about to start. The other theatergoers were also finding their seats, overstuffed containers of popcorn and boxes of Sno-Caps and Twizzlers in hand.

Massie, in a Burberry trench and D&G sunglasses, led Kristen and Bean (who was dressed in her own tiny puppy trench from Bark Jacobs) to a row near the back. She slid into the seat on the end and scanned the theater to confirm that she didn't know a single soul sitting in the orange reclining chairs. The Pretty Committee was otherwise accounted for—Dylan was having dinner with her mom, and Alicia was at dance practice—but you couldn't be too sure.

"I don't know," Massie said. "Maybe because your average is already ninety-eight?"

Kristen shrug-blushed and sank into the plush seat.

In order to convince Kristen to join her, Massie had told her the movie was for extra credit. And she wasn't completely lying. She *had* brought Kristen here for educational purposes. Though this education had nothing to do with school.

It was now T-minus one day until lip touchdown, and Massie was nearing panic mode. She had watched movie kiss after movie kiss on YouTube. But the theater's enormous high-def screen would make it a much more effective teaching tool. And who better to learn kissing *en français* from than the people who invented it?

Besides, the rest of the audience was almost all couples, which meant Massie would be able to observe other daters in their natural habitats. By spying on a couple in the "wild," Massie could notate and memorize how to act when she and Landon were out on their own date.

The crystal-sconced lights dimmed, and a hush fell over the theater. The screen switched from an ad about a wine-tasting movie to a warning for theatergoers to be quiet and silence their cell phones. Massie folded her D&G glasses and replaced them with a pair of sleek silver binoculars.

"What are those for?" Kristen whispered.

"To see the subtitles better," Massie whisper-hissed back. "Now, shhh! It's starting."

The film began with a shot of a dark forest in the south of France. On the screen flashed the words LIAISONS DIABOLIQUES. A silky-voiced narrator set the scene in French, and white, block-lettered subtitles appeared at the bottom of the screen.

"Wait!" whispered Kristen, horrified. "Will Madame Vallon still give us extra credit even though we don't have to translate?"

"Of course," Massie said. "But be quiet. I need to focus."

She trained her binoculars on a couple near the front. The guy had a frizzy blond 'fro and wore horn-rimmed glasses. The girl barely had enough hair to fill out her ponytail. They were feeding each other Jujubes, and the guy kept pretending to bite the girl's finger off. Massie wrinkled her nose.

Quel désastre.

She turned toward another couple in matching crocheted winter hats. They were sharing a bag of granola and a hummus sandwich, which they'd obviously made at home and smuggled in.

Horreur!

For a moment, Massie gave up her search and watched the movie as the heroine, Genevieve, appeared on-screen. With her pert, upturned nose and long dark curls, she looked like Christina Ricci's French younger sister. She wore a white dress and clutched a textbook to her chest as she made her way home from school. Dusk fell over the rolling landscape, and day quickly morphed into night just as Genevieve reached the edge of the forbidding woods. She crossed herself anxiously as she passed gnarled, ancient limbs that seemed as though they wanted to reach out and grab her. As soon as she made it safely inside the white clapboard house on the other side of the forest, two glowing eyes appeared in the darkness and the shadow of Olav, a 313-year-old Norwegian vampire, stepped out from behind a fat oak tree. In his arms was the body of a young girl, two prominent, bloody teeth marks imprinted in her lifeless neck.

Kristen gasped. Bean hid her head in the crook of Massie's arm. Massie just rolled her eyes. Vampires were so passé.

The scene changed to show Genevieve in a discotheque with her friends. A boy in dark wash jeans and a white button-down shirt—the picture of innocent teenage hawtness—emerged from the crowd just as Genevieve ordered a Coke from the bartender. The boy swooped in to pay for it and introduced himself as Jean-Luc, a budding poet. Genevieve shook his outstretched hand. "My, what cold hands you have," she commented. The camera panned in for a close-up of Jean-Luc's eyes. They smoldered with intensity.

Massie clutched her arm rest. Was it smooch time already?

Mais non. Genevieve merely took her Coke and rejoined her friends. Jean-Luc gazed longingly after her, then scribbled a short love poem in a small leather notebook he pulled from his jeans pocket.

Massie scanned the theater crowd again with her binoculars. Frizzy curls. *No.* Gelled spikes. *No.* Bedhead. *No.* Heidi braids. *Definitely not.* And . . . ah! Just two rows in front of them and one seat to the right, a girl with long, blond Gisele hair sat next to a boy whose mane was almost as perfectly shaggy as Landon's. The girl wore a headband and a plaid jumper, and the boy wore a Brooks Brothers blazer and scarf. They were a few years older—high school juniors or seniors, maybe—and were leaning in toward each other.

Voila!

Massie activated the voice recorder on her iPhone and

raised it to her lips. "Notes from the field, part one," she whispered. Little bars rose and fell, calibrating her volume. "Test subjects sit close but not too close to one another."

"Did you say something?" Kristen asked out of the side of her mouth, her eyes glued to the screen.

"I'm taking notes for extra credit."

Kristen gave a *wish-I'd-thought-of-that* frown.

On the screen, Jean-Luc asked Genevieve to dance. She flashed him a luminous smile, but instead of leading him to the dance floor, she took him to a utility closet at the back of the club. Once they were alone, he leaned close, as if mesmerized by her clear blue eyes. She leaned in too, like she was getting ready to lip-kiss.

Massie clutched her iPhone in anticipation. But then, suddenly, Genevieve held up a cross that she'd been hiding in her dress pocket. Jean-Luc hissed at her, his front teeth elongating into fangs.

"Ehmavampire!" Kristen gasped. "I so did *not* see that coming."

Unfazed, Genevieve pulled a vial of holy water from her pocket and tossed it on Jean-Luc, and he collapsed to the floor with a *thunk*. His leather-bound *cahier* followed with a *thud*.

Gisele Hair buried her face in her date's shoulder.

Massie bent over her iPhone. "Female test subject uses fear at a scary event as an excuse to get closer to male test subject."

In the row in front of them, a woman with salt-and-pepper hair turned around and *shhh*ed Massie.

"YOU shhhh!" Massie glared back and pointed to the screen. "We're trying to watch the movie."

On-screen, the heroine gave a quick glance around before staking Jean-Luc through the heart with a pencil she pulled from one of the shelves in the closet. Then, with a devil-may-care smile, she disappeared down the hallway and out into the night.

The scene dissolved into a foggy evening. A thin man with straight blond hair and chiseled features—Olav, the vampire—drove a car down a narrow, winding path, when suddenly a figure dashed out in the middle of the road. He swerved to avoid it, then braked sharply to see what he had come close to hitting.

"It's warm in the car," the antihero said in French as he pulled up beside Genevieve.

Bean yawned.

"Ah-greed," Massie whispered. It was no wonder French people had invented kissing. They had probably come up with it to pass the time during their snoozefest movies.

A few rows in front of them, the female test subject was feeding the male test subject popcorn a few kernels at a time. Occasionally the girl would reach out and brush the popcorn crumbs from his cheek. Massie pictured Landon's mouth being that close to her fingers and felt her neurons flash down her spine, strobe light–fast.

The male test subject finished a final mouthful of popcorn and then put his arm around the female test subject, who yawned and put her head on his shoulder.

"Female test subject uses the excuse of being tired to lean against the male test subject—who, on second thought, needs a haircut."

"Ix-nay on the ommentary-cay," said Kristen. She motioned to the screen with her chin.

Massie closed down the recorder and opened her iPhone notepad instead.

Uch. Couldn't *someone* get to kissing already? Massie let her mind wander to thoughts of Landon. How his eyes crinkled whenever he was in the sun. The way his dark curls tickled the edges of his ears. How he half smiled whenever his pug, Bark, licked him. How he had opened the door for Massie to his mom's couture dog boutique, Bark Jacobs. How he liked to put his arm around Massie whenever other boys tried to flirt with her. And how waves of crushness flowed between them whenever they were together.

A quiet giggle two rows up brought Massie's attention back to Gisele Hair and The Mane. The female test subject leaned in close and whispered something to the male. Then she leaned back the tiniest bit and nodded. Their lips were *almost* touching.

Use whispering to increase closeness, Massie typed into her iPhone notepad.

The test couple was leaning in: 3 . . . 2 . . . 1 . . .

"Kiss should begin slowly," Massie whispered.

The male test subject opened his mouth slightly. And then wider. And wider. The female test subject opened her mouth even wider than his and stuck her tongue all the way out of her mouth, like she was getting ready for a throat culture at the doctor's office. Then, suddenly, they smashed their faces together like two trains crashing at top speed.

Massie gasped and almost dropped her phone.

The female test subject brought her hands up to both sides of the male test subject's face. He moved his jaw up and down, like she was a double cheeseburger. And she made the same lip-smacking, slurping noises Layne had made when she'd dared herself to eat a whole watermelon without using her hands.

And that's when Massie saw The Mane pass a blue wad of gum to Gisele Hair *with his tongue*.

Massie clutched her iPhone. This was awl wrong! This wasn't sweet or romantic. This was . . . gross!

A second later the couple pulled apart. The male's tongue hung out of his mouth, like he was a Doberman after a long run. The girl chewed on the piece of gum, then wiped her slobbery mouth with the back of her sleeve.

And then they went back in for more.

Massie tasted the Nutz Over Chocolate Luna bar she'd eaten on the ride over. *Ehmabarf!*

The couple had looked so normal, with their fashionable outfits and adequate haircuts, but they were chewed-gum-sharing freaks!

Massie put her hand over Bean's eyes, hoping her pup had not suffered long-term eye damage.

On the screen, Genevieve was sneaking into Olav's motel room. Pale moonlight splashed across his face as he lay in a coffin, eyes wide open. She lowered her face down over his.

They stared into each others' eyes and opened their mouths ever so slightly, in perfect unison.

Maybe this movie wasn't so useless after all . . .

Notes from the field, part two, Massie typed into her phone. *Stare into eyes. Part lips in unison, no more than three-quarters of an inch. Ideally, female test subject will have stray lock of hair or tear on her face so male test subject has something to lovingly brush away . . .*

There was simply too much occurring to type, so she switched her iPhone to video and held it up.

On-screen, Olav, with his centuries of lip-kissing experience, sat up in his coffin and cupped Genevieve's chin in his hand. Tears sparkled in her eyes as she admitted that she'd only ever kissed one boy before and she'd never even dreamed of kissing a vampire. "Do not worry, *ma petite cherie,*" Olav said in a husky voice. "I will not bite."

As the actors touched lips, Massie smiled and scratched Bean's ears. From where she was sitting, that didn't look too hard. Stare, part lips, initiate kiss, tilt head. It was exactly the same maneuver she'd used with Derrington. Maybe kissing an older man was like kissing an older vampire—and like kissing a regular old eighth-grader. So long as lips were involved, it was all pretty much the same thing.

"It's so romantic!" Kristen whispered.

Just then, an ah-dorable little pug pranced on-screen. Bean sat straight up and started whimpering. Loudly.

"Shhh, Bean," Massie whispered. "We're trying to watch a movie."

Two rows up, Gisele Hair turned around. She gasped when she saw Massie's iPhone held up at eye level. She leaned over to her boyfriend, who had just popped a new piece of gum in his mouth.

The Mane turned around too, and scowled. "Are we going to end up on YouTube or something? What if my girlfriend sees?"

"Ew, gawd," Massie said. "I'm filming the *movie*. And so should you. Your technique needs help."

Gisele Hair narrowed her eyes at Massie. Then she grabbed her jacket and flounced up the aisle, The Mane at her heels.

A moment later Massie felt a tap on her shoulder. A pimply movie usher dressed in a red polyester blazer hovered at her side.

"Excuse me, ma'am," the usher said. "Were you videotaping a couple?"

"Ew, no!" Massie exclaimed. "Just the movie." She pointed to the screen, where Genevieve and Olav were engaged in a passionate kiss *bonjour*. She held her iPhone up so she wouldn't miss it.

"Ma'am," he said, shuffling his pleather-loafered feet against the tacky theater floor. "Bootlegging is a federal offense."

"Puh-lease. Bootleg jeans? Maybe two years ago, but if fashion crimes were really illegal, then . . ." She looked pointedly at his blazer.

"He's talking about filming the movie," Kristen whispered.

"Oh," Massie whispered back.

The usher adjusted the sleeves of his jacket and took a few steps toward her. "Also, ma'am, we don't allow dogs." He pointed the beam of his flashlight toward Bean. She quivered in Massie's lap, probably frightened by how ugly the usher's outfit was. Bean had a serious polyester phobia. "We're going to have to ask you to leave the theater now."

"But . . ." Massie pointed to the lip-kissing couple on-screen. "The movie isn't over!"

The usher didn't budge. He just crossed his arms. "Ma'am, please don't make me call security."

"Fine," Massie said. She turned to Kristen. "Let's go!"

They walked up the black-and-white–swirled carpet and passed Gisele Hair and The Mane, who'd relocated to the very back row. "Stalker," Gisele Hair hissed.

Massie stopped short in her Tory Burch Gigi snow boots. "Excuse me, but are you pregnant?"

Gisele Hair's hand flew to her stomach. The Mane's jaw dropped so fast, his gum fell out of his mouth. "No," Gisele Hair snapped.

"Then don't kid yourself."

While Kristen snickered softly, Massie tucked Bean under her arm like a football and marched outside to the snowy curb to phone Isaac to pick them up. Another movie had just released, and people in puffy coats and fUggs streamed into the parking lot.

Kristen sighed and snapped her lime green earmuffs over her lobes. "I bet we won't get the extra credit now."

But Massie just smiled and patted the lip kiss–containing iPhone in her jacket pocket. *Maybe you won't,* she thought. *But I will.*

After waving goodbye to Isaac and giving him strict instructions to wait for her five blocks away, Massie checked the final version of her Landon Lip Kiss outfit in the narrow windows on either side of the Cranes' front door. It was perfect: a D&G black corset under a gray Theory blazer, paired with a dark denim pair of skinnys. It said, *I'm easy, breezy, beautiful, and lip-kissing an older man is no big deal to me.* Plus, the thick corset fabric was just the thing to muffle a loudly pounding heart. To amp up the flirt factor, she wore four-inch stacked Betsey Johnson heels. Pink toes peeked out from under her jeans.

"Okay, Bean, this is it." She pressed the doorbell, which was brass and in the shape of a dog bone. They sold the bells exclusively at Bark Jacobs, and all the profits went to PETA.

A moment later, a smiling Mrs. Crane opened the door and ushered Massie inside the slate-floored entryway. Her dark hair fell in loose curls over her shoulders, and her aqua eyes shone. "So good to see you, Massie! I hope you like mocha buttercream cake." She kissed Massie lightly on each cheek, then knelt down to eye level with Bean and handed her a box. "And I hope *you* like macaroons!"

Bean lick-thanked Mrs. Crane's arm and sniffed the box of imported Parisian puppy-macaroons. Massie opened the box so Bean could see the flavors: lemon, raspberry, and vanilla. Each was decorated with a tiny dog bone in real gold leaf.

"*Arf!*" Bark Obama came scurrying from the kitchen into the parlor. The moment Bean saw him, she abandoned her macaroons, and the two dogs launched into a joyful barking and sniffing frenzy. They yelped and hopped, then gave each other lip kiss after lip kiss. Clearly neither had felt the need to practice for hours ahead of time, and clearly neither was nervous even though they hadn't seen each other since before Thanksgiving.

Massie took a breath. If only it could be so easy for their owners.

"Landon's in his room," Mrs. Crane said, pointing to the stairs. "Let him know I'm cutting the birthday cake in ten minutes."

"Okay," Massie said, pushing her hand against her chest where her heart was trying to pound its way right out. She'd never actually been to Landon's room, but she knew he had an olive-green duvet, chocolate-brown throw pillows, and a John Mayer poster over his bed, thanks to the SnoopDawg dog collar camera she'd used to spy on him in the early days of their crushship.

She forced herself to walk calmly to the staircase, timing her steps to the beat of Fergie's "Big Girls Don't Cry." She faux-casually examined the black-and-white family photos on the scarlet walls, like climbing a set of black-lacquered stairs to lip-kiss an older man was something she did every day—no more unique than re-glossing or debating the merits of bronzer versus spray tanning.

When she reached the top of the stairs, she paused, trying to remember everything she'd learned from *Liaisons Diaboliques*. She had watched the video on her iPhone at least a dozen times and had spent hours practicing. But suddenly, her mouth was as dry as the desert they'd studied in geography that morning—only she couldn't remember the name of it because she had been too busy worrying about kissing Landon.

She took a step into the hallway. Downstairs, Bark and Bean barked happily and Mrs. Crane let out a throaty laugh. The upstairs was also painted red, but the black-and-white photos here were of Landon and his parents, starting from when he was a chubby baby with elephant rolls to the HART (hawt, alpha, rich, and toned) ninth-grader he was now.

Then she was at Landon's bedroom door, which had a paw-printed HAPPY BIRTHDAY! sign taped across it. Inhaling a final calming breath, she took out her secret weapon: Glossip Girl's Vixen. It was a sheer, jasmine-scented gloss, the perfect combination of silky and smooth.

And then she knocked.

"Come in!"

Landon was sitting with his back to her, facing his computer desk. He wore a black-and-gray sweater over Diesel jeans. When her eyes worked their way down to his bright green socks, she felt a crush-ing wave wash over her. Their black-and-gray outfits perfectly complemented each other's.

Before she lost her nerve, she marched right up to him and spun his chair around, reminding herself that alphas were *always* in control. Massie envisioned herself like a pair of control-top Spanx: a quivering mess on the inside, but completely contained.

"Are you ready for your birthday present?" she asked, surprised her voice wasn't shaking the way Bean did after her weekly bath.

Landon's adorable blue-green eyes widened, but before he could say anything—and before Massie lost her nerve—she reached down, grabbed both sides of his face, parted her lips, and initiated the lean-in. His arms felt warm, and he smelled of L'Homme. Then she tilted her head the exact right number of degrees to the left.

She touched her lips to his.

Her heart blared like a royal trumpeter announcing the arrival of a new lip-kissing queen. She was doing it! She was finally lip-kissing a ninth-grader!

But to her surprise, Landon's lips were as stiff as the Massiequin's had been. When she'd kissed Derrington, his mouth had always felt soft, like overripe green grapes, while Landon's was orange-rind hard. Was he nervous? Was he less experienced than she'd suspected?

Ehmagawd, thought Massie.

Was she doing it wrong?

Her amber eyes snapped open. His blue ones were staring back at her. She'd learned in art class that if you drew the whites on all sides of the iris, your subjects wouldn't look natural—they'd look scared. And that's when she realized: Landon looked . . . panicked.

Her mind spun faster than the Truth or Dare app on her iPhone. Was there something on her face? Was it possible he didn't like the taste of the Glossip Girl? Had she slobbered on him?

Then, from behind Landon, Massie heard a wobbly, older voice ask, "And who is this, dear?"

Huh?

Slowly, Massie peeked around Landon and came face-to-screen with his desktop. And right there on the open screen were two very sweet-looking old people, smiling thinly. One of them waved.

"Grandmom, Gramps, this is Massie Block, the girl I told you about." Landon turned to her, the look of panic not yet gone from his face. "Massie, I was just G-video-chatting them to thank them for my birthday present."

"Oh, my," said his grandfather. "She sure is . . . fast."

Fast? Was that old people for *skanky*?

Landon's grandmother frowned, the lines in her face as deep as the Grand Canyon. "Landon, I thought you said she was a *nice* girl."

Massie felt like the pores on her face had exploded into flames. Her brain was functioning on slo-mo, and she'd lost all feeling in her lips. Through the haze she decided she could a) pretend she was May-see, Massie's vixeny twin sister, b) start choking and claim the kiss was simply life-saving mouth-to-mouth resuscitation, c) laugh it off, as if she broadcast her lip kisses over the Internet *awl* the time, or d) . . .

RUN.

Without another glance at Landon, she spun on her Betsey Johnson heels, scrambled into the hallway, and clacked down the wooden steps—past the Zen-chic foyer, past a confused-looking Mrs. Crane (who shouted a confused "You're not staying for cake?"), all the way out to the flagstone front walk. It wasn't until she was halfway down the driveway that she realized she'd forgotten Bean.

"Arggg!" she whisper-groaned. But going back into the Crane household would be like choosing to shop at Payless: It was never going to happen. So she sent ESP waves to her pup, hoping Bean understood that she'd send Isaac to retrieve her in the morning.

As she glanced over her shoulder at the three-story brick house, for one brief moment she dared to dream that Landon might come after her with Bean in his arms, Kelly Clarkson's "My Life Would Suck Without You" blaring from his iPhone, shouting for her to come back inside and eat cake and be her forever-crush.

But then she reached the end of the driveway.

And then the end of the street.

And then the end of the next one.

And the only thing following Massie was the sinking realization that her life was over.

CURRENT STATE OF THE UNION

IN	OUT
Diss Kiss	Aqua-Bliss Kiss
Puppy love	People love
Granny cam	Nanny cam

It was Tuesday evening, one day after picking up the roaches at Karma Chameleon and T-minus ten minutes from placing them in their intended location. The Block Estate was dark and forbidding.

"You're positive no one's home?" Layne asked.

"We're in the clear until at least eight thirty." Earlier that evening, Claire had brought Isaac some of her mom's famous hot chocolate and casually asked what he had on tap for the evening. After dropping Kendra and William at a fundraiser at the country club at seven fifteen, he'd said, he would be escorting Massie to Landon Crane's house for birthday cake, all the while waiting five blocks away in case Bean got a case of doggie-sushi and had to be taken home. Then he'd narrowed his bushy brows at Claire and asked why she'd wanted to know. "No reason," she'd squeaked. "Just making conversation."

Now, Claire stood in the hard-packed snow directly below her former alpha's bedroom. For a second, she literally froze—from guilt, not the cold. The temperature was in the teens, and her breath puffed from her lips in a steady stream. An owl hooted accusingly overhead, and the bare, snow-covered brambles in the flower beds seemed to shake their branches at her in disapproval. Even Massie's darkened windows one story up seemed to reflect the darkness in Claire's soul. But then Claire reminded herself who had bugged whom first, and she handed the habitat up to Layne with more bravado then she felt.

Layne reached out one big-yellow-gloved hand from her perch and took a step up the ladder that was leaned against the outer wall of Massie's house. Then she checked to make sure her harnesses and clamps were secure.

Claire and Layne had dressed themselves in black from head to spray-painted Keds. Layne had even painted black zebra stripes under her eyes, like a football player. She had tons of trapeze equipment at home from circus camp, so she had insisted on being the active agent in this mission. She wore a miner's helmet with a headlamp, safety goggles, a pair of climbing gloves, and an intricate system of harnesses and carabiner clips. She looked like Lady Gaga on tour. It seemed like kind of a lot, considering she was just going to be climbing up one story on a very secure-looking ladder. And the harnesses and carabiners were attached only to themselves. But Layne had insisted it was much safer and more official this way.

"Let's practice the bird sound again," Layne said.

Claire's role was more avian than active. She was to stand watch and make a bird sound if anyone came near.

"Well?"

"Cer-ooooo!" Claire whispered, feeling silly. "Cer-ooooo!"

"Well done," said Layne. "Don't forget. One *cer-ooooo* for Massie. Two *cer-ooooo*s for anyone else."

"Why can't we use the same *cer-ooooo*? It's kind of a lot to remember." Claire glanced anxiously at her blue Baby

G-Shock watch. It was the exact same color as Cam's left eye, the one that she knew would look at her in disappointment when he found out what she had done. After hearing about their revenge plot, he'd told her not to go through with it. "Don't stoop to her level," he'd said. But this was *war*. And Massie had launched the first offensive.

Layne was saying, "Because, Kuh-lu-less, if it's Massie I will have one story prepared, and for anyone else I will have another, equally moving story prepared."

"A story prepared for what you're doing in Massie's room with a box full of bugs?" A gummy foot–shaped lump formed in the back of Claire's throat, but she did her best to swallow it.

Layne fiddled with a metallic purple safety clip. "You've obviously never broken into anyone's house before. Besides, no one will be home for hours, re-*mem*-ber?"

Claire's teeth chattered. "I know, I know."

With that Layne began to climb the ladder slowly, holding the habitat with one hand. "Look at me!" she whisper-shouted from the third rung. "I can see for miles. Look, there's OCD! There's the firehouse! There's Ma and Pa."

Claire giggled in spite of herself. She held the ladder steady, bracing against the reverberations of Layne's Keds as they slammed against each step. But Layne had barely reached the fifth rung when, in what seemed like slow motion, she started to sway like a piece of overcooked pasta. She moved to grasp the sides of the ladder with both hands . . . and she let. Go. Of. The. Habitat.

"Ahhh!" Claire screamed as the plastic box bounced off

her head. "Cer-ooooo! Cer-ooooo!" She squeezed her eyes shut, scared to open them and see what she knew to be true: Multiplying pincer bugs were burrowing into her black BDG sweatshirt, feasting on her pale skin, while the crickets left a microscopic trail of insect poo along her hair part, like a stylist applying highlights. *Karma!* Claire's inner voice screamed at her as she doubled over and held her knees, breathing deeply into what their yoga teacher called the "child's pose."

"Claire!" Layne's voice sounded from above as her sneakers squeaked down the ladder.

"Are they on me?" Claire asked, swatting herself hysterically.

"Oh no . . ." Layne gasped. Claire looked up just as Layne hopped off the bottom rung of the ladder. But one of her carabiners had snagged the ladder's rung. It toppled like a silver domino. In the silence of the night, the crash sounded louder than a foghorn.

"Layne!" Claire shouted at her friend, who was trapped beneath it. "Are you okay?"

"Hurry!" Layne shouted back. The bugs were scurrying in opposite directions.

Taking a deep breath, Claire bent down and, as quickly as she could she—*yuck, yuck, yuck, yuck, yuck, yuck, yuck, yuck!*—picked up the bugs and tossed them into the habitat before she could feel their creepy-crawly little legs poke her through her mittens. She locked the habitat, then helped disentangle Layne from the ladder. Together, the two propped it back up against the house.

"Do you think anyone heard?" Layne asked, opening her eyes wide as she scanned the backyard for movement.

"All the lights are still off," Claire pointed out. "So I think we're clear."

"Phew! Although," Layne said, holding up one yellow-gloved finger in the air, "I would like to point out that your use of *cer-ooooo* in that situation was not entirely correct."

Claire shook her head as Layne slowly but surely started back up the rungs. When she finally reached the top, she pushed on the windowpane. Once. Twice. "Cer-ooo, cer-ooo!" she whisper-screamed.

"Is someone in there?" Claire cried out, the muscles in her legs coiling, getting ready to bolt.

"It's locked."

Claire tilted her head up. The Big Dipper shone brightly in the sky like a bunch of judgmental eyes. "Are you sure?"

"Yeah, you want me to punch through the window?" Layne sounded excited. "These gloves are pretty thick. I think I could do it."

"Layne! No! I've got it covered," Claire said. "Don't go anywhere."

Pressing her back against the stone wall, Claire inched her way along the perimeter of the Block Estate. Shrubs snatched at her thighs, and tree branches smashed her in the face. She crab-slid beneath a dry evergreen.

"Achoo!" she sneezed.

"Good job!" Layne called softly from around the corner. Instead of "Bless you" or "Gesundheit," Layne liked to say,

"Good job," as in *Good job getting those germs out of your nose*. Claire rolled her eyes and shrank further into the bushes.

She made it to the Blocks' large veranda with the giant, carved-out double doors. She perched behind a large potted plant and pressed her hand against the house's stone façade. A gray brick popped open and revealed a digital keypad. She paused in front of the alarm. It had been so long since she'd used it. What was it again?

Massie's birthday?

Or Bean's?

Was it the date Massie became an official Glossip Girl black card member?

Guilt and adrenaline made her hands shake as she pressed 1–1–2–9.

The alarm let out a loud *BEEEEP* . . . then DISARMED flashed across the screen in neon red letters.

Tentatively, Claire pushed the door open.

Silence.

She opened the door a little more.

More silence.

Claire stepped into the vestibule of the Block house. There was no one in sight. Quietly, she tiptoed up the plush steps to the second floor. Looking both ways when she reached the second-floor landing, she scurried down the hall and into Massie's room. The lights were out, and she didn't dare turn them on. She stepped inside—and directly into something solid . . . and Massie-shaped.

"Massie!" Claire whisper-gasped, the smell of Passion Fruit

filling her nostrils. This was it. It was all over. Her brain let out a forlorn, silent *cer-oooo*. "I was just . . ."

But when the figure didn't let out a shrill *Kuh-laire!* Claire tentatively reached out her hand. Her fingers grazed something soft and squishy, like the foamy part of a pushup bra, but also hard, like Plexiglas. Claire laid a hand over her racing heart, relief flooding her body. *Of course. The Massiequin.*

Outside the window she saw Layne, perched on the ladder, flashing her miner's headlamp in a plea to be let in.

Claire raced across the room and opened the window.

Layne climbed in and clicked the headlamp on. "I want to do a sweep for any Massie-cams or . . ." She paused dramatically. "BUGS." She giggle-snorted into her right hand.

As Layne surveyed the room, images of former friendship with Massie flashed through Claire's brain. Gossiping on the white throw carpet about Olivia Ryan's latest nose. IM'ing with the soccer boys on Massie's MacBook. Trying on Alice + Olivia dresses in Massie's massive walk-in closet.

Claire's conscience sent Mean Girl Alert tremors through her body, and for a moment, she wondered if she should really go through with this. Massie was more scared of bugs than Demi Moore was of aging. What if she had a panic attack and turned Bella-white? And what if that panic attack induced an even worse panic attack and she got even whiter, like Bella in *Breaking Dawn*? At the very least, Massie would be really, really, *really* freaked out.

But then Claire saw a shaft of moonlight bouncing off Massie's large flat-screen TV, reminding Claire of the way light now reflected off Todd's bald head. Her resolve returned, stronger than ever. Massie had balded her brother under false pretenses and sabotaged her new friendships. She deserved to get Raided.

"All clear. No cams," Layne announced. "Ooh, a Luna bar!" She unwrapped the treat and shoved it in her mouth.

"Layne," Claire warned. "I think that's one of Bean's gourmet dog treats!"

"Huh." Layne chewed thoughtfully. "Not bad."

Claire pulled back Massie's fluffy down comforter, revealing the lavender Frette sheets. Layne undid the top latch on the bug habitat and shook the creepy-crawlies out onto the bed, where they landed with soft *kerplunk*s before scurrying in all directions.

"Go forth and conquer, you little buggers," Layne said.

Claire and Layne folded the sheets back up and tucked them into the sides of the bed so the bugs couldn't get out.

Suddenly, the sound of wheels crunching over gravel filled Claire's ears, and headlights flashed through the window. The girls jumped.

"Evacuate," Claire cried, fear constricting her throat.

Layne rushed to the window, tripping over Claire's foot in her hurry. They fell on top of each other like they were playing a spirited game of Twister.

"Get *awf* me," Layne said, her mouth shoved into the carpet.

"You get off me!" Claire rolled over and hit the side of Massie's bureau. She kicked out her leg, knocking into a metal rod on wheels. The Massiequin. "Oh no!"

The mannequin wobbled back and forth, as if taking a minute to think over its next move, then fell on top of the two girls.

"It's got me!" screeched Layne. "Save yourself, Claire! It's too late for me."

Claire righted the mannequin—which, oddly, looked like it had lip gloss on—and dragged Layne up from the floor. "Come on!"

"Cer-oooooo!" Layne whimpered. "Cer-ooooooo!"

Claire helped Layne through the window, and the two climbed quickly down to the ground below.

"Do you think she'll suspect it was us who put the bugs in her bed?" Layne asked, her green eyes wide, when her feet were pressed firmly in the snow.

"I don't know. But I do know why James Bond worked alone." Claire shoulder-bumped Layne.

Layne nodded, a look of great certainty on her face. "Totes," she said. "Because it was easier to score chicks that way." And with that Layne ran-hobbled to her bike, and with one final "Cer-ooooo!" she took off.

Fifteen minutes after the apoca-lips—although it felt more like fifteen years or fifteen seasons of *Gossip Girl*—Isaac pulled into the Blocks' driveway, and Massie's suspicion had solidified into fact. It was definitely over. Landon had not called or texted once. Not even to say he had Bean.

Massie's stomach clenched, like she'd been kicked in the gut with a steel-toed stiletto. She'd never been this mortified, not even when Alicia had informed her that *thong* was nawt just another word for *flip-flop*. Within a matter of hours, it would be around the high school *and* the local old-age homes. Landon's grandparents were obviously very tech-savvy. The next seventy years of her life would be plagued by this one horrible accident. She wondered how hard it was to get into witness—or in this case, kissness—protection and secure a new identity for herself.

Massie got out of the car, wiping the tears off her mascara-streaked cheeks. A warm yellow light was glowing from Claire's bedroom window in the guesthouse. Massie felt a sudden overwhelming urge to run over there, knock on Claire's window, and spill her guts about the kisstastrophe. Instead, she turned and trudged into her house.

The house was dark—her parents were still out—but for

some reason the alarm system was down. She reactivated it, then just stood there breathing for a moment, thinking about how her anxiety cloud had just turned into a bluish-black tornado.

She ran up to her room, turned on the anxiety audiobook, and collapsed onto her white shag carpet.

"MAINTAIN PERSPECTIVE," the voice told her. "THINGS ARE NEVER AS BAD AS THEY SEEM."

Massie wondered if maybe, just maybe, her kiss wasn't as bad as she thought. Maybe she had to maintain perspective, to find the good in her situation. Maybe her kiss was more similar to the famous kisses than she realized—it was, if nothing else, dramatic.

She reviewed her list mentally.

The Mys Kiss, in *Spider-Man,* for example, was similar because . . . well, Massie *had* been at sort of an awkward angle, which was kind of like how Spidey had been upside down. Although, it would have been more similar had Kirsten Dunst pulled Spidey's face mask all the way down by accident during the kiss, knocking him off the wall and into a pile of cardboard crates.

The Risk Kiss in *Twilight* was similar because kissing in front of your crush's grandparents *was* risky. Although the Risk Kiss would have been a little more similar if afterward Bella had actually died. Of embarrassment. The way Massie had.

The Diss Kiss at the VMAs was definitely similar insofar as only one of the participants in her kiss had actually been ready to kiss at that moment. Although the kisses would have been more similar if Kristen Stewart and Robert Pattinson had knocked foreheads and then he had run away screaming and fallen off the stage.

The Aqua-Bliss Kiss, truthfully, wasn't similar to hers at awl, except for the fact that Massie had cried a lot afterward, so her face was just as wet as Rachel McAdams's and Ryan Gosling's faces after kissing in the rain.

The Hiss Kiss on *Gossip Girl* was similar because both kisses involved onlookers. The kiss would have been more similar, though, if when Serena kissed Nate at a party to make his cougar girlfriend jealous, it turned out that all of Nate's family members and the family members of the cougar girlfriend were watching on video chat.

Oh gawd, who was she kidding? Her kiss belonged in a category all its own: the I'm Never Going to Get Over This Kiss. Oh gawd. The high-schoolers would laugh at her. The middle-schoolers would no longer look up to her. And the grade-schoolers would see her as a public service announcement for what nawt to do.

Massie's iPhone buzzed loudly.

Landon?! Maybe he was telling her that he'd tucked Bean in for the night. Or that, after some thought, he'd decided he had liked the kiss and wanted to video all their kisses.

Frantically, she dumped her handbag on her bedspread. Out fell two Glossip Girl tubes, a case of peppermint Altoids, the ticket stub to *Liaisons Diaboliques,* a mascara-soaked tissue, and finally her iPhone. A text glowed on the screen.

Alicia: Ready to kiss and tell?

"Ugh!" Massie immediately powered down her phone and stuck it in her desk drawer. The only thing that could help now—short of a time machine—was sleep. She slipped into her lavender silk pajamas, then climbed onto her bed, and hid under the soft covers.

"Bean, is that you?" Massie called groggily an hour later, awaking to a light tickle on her leg.

"Arf?" Bean responded from her perch on her doggy bed, a clean three feet away from the tickle on Massie's leg.

Confused, Massie sat up and snapped on her bedside light. She pulled back the purple duvet and—

*"AHHHHHHHHHHHHHHHHHHHHHHHHHHHHHHHHHH-
HHHHHHHHHHHHHHHHHHHHHHHHHHHHHHHHHHHHH-
HHHHHHHHHHHHHHHHHHHHHHHHHHHHHHHHHHHHH-
HHHHHHHHHHHHHHHHHHHHHHHHHHHHHHHHHHHHH-
HHHHHHHHHHHHHHHHHHHHHHHHHHHHHHHHHHHHH-
HHHHHHHHHHHHHHHHHHHHHHHHHHHHHHHHHHHHH-
HHHHHHHHHHHHHHHHHHHHHHHHHHHHHHHHHHHHH-
HHHHHHHHHHHHHHHHHHHHHHHHHHHHHHHHHHHHH-
HHHHHHHHHHHHHHHHHHHHHHHHHHHHHHHHHHHHH-
HHHHHHHHHHHHHHHHHHHHHHHHHHHHHHHHHHHHH-
HHHHHHHHHHHHHHHHHHHHHHHHHHHHHHHHHHHHH-
HHHHHHHHHHHHHHHHHHHHHHHHHHHHHHHHHHHHH-
HHHHHHHHHHHHHHHHHHHHHHHHHHHHHHHHHHHHH-
HHHHHHHHHHHHHHHHHHHHHHHHHHHHHHHHHHHHH-
HHHHHHHHHHHHHHHHHHHHHHHHHHHHHHHHHHHHH-
HHHHHHHHHHHHHHHHHHHHHHHHHHHHHHHHHHHHH-*

HHHHHHHHHHHHHHHHHHHHHHHHHHHHHHHHHHHHHHHHHHHH-
HHHHHHHHHHHHHHHHHHHHHHHHHHHHHHHHHHHHHHHHHHHH-
HHHHHHHHHHHHHHHHHHHHHHHHHHHHHHHHHHHHHHHHHHHH-
HHHHHHHHHHHHHHHHHHHHHHHHHHHHHHHHHHHHHHHHHHHH-
HHHHHHHHHHHHHHHHHHHHHHHHHHHHHHHHHHHHHHHHHHHH-
HHHHHHHHHHHHHHHHHHHHHHHHHHHHHHHHHHHHHHHHHHHH-
HHHHHHHHHHHHHHHHHHHHHHHHHHHHHHHHHHHHHHHHHHHH-
HHHHHHHHHHHHHHHHHHHHHHHHHHHHHHHHHHHHHHHHHHHH-
HHHHHHHHHHHHHHHHHHHHHHHHHHHHHHHHHHHHHHHHHHHH-
HHHHHHHHHHHHHHHHHHHHHHHHHHHHHHHHHHHHHHHHHHHH-
HHHHHHHHHHHHHHHHHHHHHHHHHHHHHHHHHHHHHHHHHHHH-
HHHHHHHHHHHHHHHHHHHHHHHHHHHHHHHHHHHHHHHHHHHH-
HHHHHHHHHHHHHHHHHHHHHHHHHHHHHHHHHHHHHHHHHHHH-
HHHHHHHHHHHHHHHHHHHHHHHHHHHHHHHHHHHHHHHHHHHH-
HHHHHHHHHHHHHHHHHHHHHHHHHHHHHHHHHHHHHHHHHHHH-
HHHHHHHHHHHHHHHHHHHHHHHHHHHHHHHHHHHHHHHHHHHH-
HHHHHHHHHHHHHHHHHHHHHHHHHHHHHHHHHHHHHHHHHHHH-
HHHHHHHHHHHHHHHHHHHHHHHHHHHHHHHHHHHHHHHHHHHH-
HHHHHHHHHHHHHHHHHHHHHHHHHHHHHHHHHHHHHHHHHHHHH-
HHHHHHHHHHHHHHHHHH!"

"AHHHHHHHHHHHHHHHHHHHHHHHHHHHHHHHHHHHHH-
HHHHHHHHHHHHHHHHHHHHHHHHHHHHHHHHHHHHHHH-
HHHHHHHHHHHHHHHHHHHHHHHHHHHHHHHHHHHHHHH-
HHHHHHHHHHHHHHHHHHHHHHHHHHHHHHHHHHHHHHH-
HHHHHHHHHHHHHHHHHHHHHHHHHHHHHHHHHHHHHHH-
HHHHHHHHHHHHHHHHHHHHHHHHHHHHHHHHHHHHHHH-
HHHHHHHHHHHHHHHHHHHHHHHHHHHHHHHHHHHHHHH-
HHHHHHHHHHHHHHHHHHHHHHHHHHHHHHHHHHHHHHH-
HHHHHHHHHHHHHHHHHHHHHHHHHHHHHHHHHHHHHHH-
HHHHHHHHHHHHHHHHHHHHHHHHHHHHHHHHHHHHHHH-
HHHHHHHHHHHHHHHHHHHHHHHHHHHHHHHHHHHHHHH-
HHHHHHHHHHHHHHHHHHHHHHHHHHHHHHHHHHHHHHH-
HHHHHHHHHHHHHHHHHHHHHHHHHHHHHHHHHHHHHHH-
HHHHHHHHHHHHHHHHHHHHHHHHHHHHHHHHHHHHHHH-
HHHHHHHHHHHHHHHHHHHHHHHHHHHHHHHHHHHHHHH-
HHHHHHHHHHHHHHHHHHHHHHHHHHHHHHHHHHHHHHH-
HHHHHHHHHHHHHHHHHHHHHHHHHHHHHHHHHHHHHHH-
HHHHHHHHHHHHHHHHHHHHHHHHHHHHHHHHHHHHHHH-
HHHHHHHHHHHHHHHHHHHHHHHHHHHHHHHHHHHHHHH-
HHHHHHHHHHHHHHHHHHHHHHHHHHHHHHHHHHHHHHH-
HHHHHHHHHHHHHHHHHHHHHHHHHHHHHHHHHHHHHHH-
HHHHHHHHHHHHHHHHHHHHHHHHHHHHHHHHHHHHHHH-
HHHHHHHHHHHHHHHHHHHHHHHHHHHHHHHHHHHHHHH-

HHHHHHHHHHHHHHHHHHHHHHHHHHHHHHHHHHHHHHH-
HHHHHHHHHHHHHHHHHHHHHHHHHHHHHHHHHHHHHHH-
HHHHHHHHHHHHHHHHHHHHHHHHHHHHHHHHHHHHHHH-
HHHHHHHHHHHHHHHHHH!"

Claire's mouth spread into a super-wide smile. She threw off her covers and ran to the window. Every single light in the Block house flicked on in rapid succession, from Massie's room at the second-floor right corner all the way to the library on the bottom-floor left, as though the entire house were doing the wave.

Claire felt a wave of her own. It was either guilt or victory. She was too tired to tell.

As Massie continued to shriek, Claire quickly settled into her desk and video-chatted Layne.

Layne appeared on the screen, sitting in a high-backed chair and wearing what appeared to be an old-fashioned smoking jacket (or was that her bathrobe?). She was drinking something yellow and creamy-looking from an over-sized brandy snifter. On the table next to her was a carton of eggnog-flavored rice milk (her newest obsession). A big stuffed animal—a cat—was in her lap, and she was stroking it. "Well, hello, Kuh-laire," she said in a low voice. She raised the glass up toward Claire like she was toasting her.

Claire giggled, then held the laptop up to the window. "Hear that?"

Layne smiled a huge eggnoggy smile and then wiped her mouth.

The scream continued, getting louder by the second.

*"AHHHHHHHHHHHHHHHHHHHHHHHHHHHHHHHHHHHHHH-
HHHHHHHHHHHHHHHHHHHHHHHHHHHHHHHHHHHHHHH-
HHHHHHHHHHHHHHHHHHHHHHHHHHHHHHHHHHHHHHH-
HHHHHHHHHHHHHHHHHHHHHHHHHHHHHHHHHHHHH!"*

"Sounds like she ran out back and . . ." Claire peered into the dark backyard. "And she's running around the pool?"

"A little night swimming perhaps?" Layne refilled her glass.

Claire snickered.

"What do you think her face looked like when she saw them?" Layne said.

"Like this." Claire made a goofy monkey face into the camera of her laptop.

Layne snorted rice milk onto the screen. "No, this!" she said, crossing her eyes and puffing out her cheeks. "Yee-gads. She's still screaming. You weren't kidding about the whole not-liking-bugs business."

"Guess this means Mission Bedbugs is a success," said Claire.

"And how!" Layne put down her brandy snifter, and the two girls high-fived their screens.

A moment later Claire signed off and went back to her window.

The entire Block family was out on the front lawn now. Mr. and Mrs. Block were in big, fluffy bathrobes, holding giant mugs of something steaming. Massie was in her silk Calvin pajamas and was holding on to her mother, whimpering.

Claire watched as, a few minutes later, Isaac came outside, still wearing his black driving outfit. He wrapped a thick blanket around Massie's shoulders and then said something to Mr. Block, who nodded. Eventually, they began to file back inside. Claire figured Massie wouldn't return to her room that night. If she knew her former alpha at all, she'd insist on sleeping in one of the bathtubs, a can of bug spray clutched to her chest.

For a moment, Claire felt bad for her former friend. Yes, Massie had bugged her first, but Claire was more resilient than Massie. She'd had to deal with hardships, like moving to a new town and living with a mean queen bee and battling sale seekers at Marshalls and overcoming adversity to rise to the top of OCD's social strata. But Massie has never had to do any of that. She'd always been popular and rich. What was it that Claire's mom always said? What doesn't kill you just makes you stronger.

A little voice at the back of Claire's brain whispered that "she did it first" wasn't a good enough reason, that Claire was just trying to justify her actions, that maybe she shouldn't have exacted such a terrible revenge on Massie. But Claire shushed it.

And with that, she flipped off her light, climbed into her own soft, bug-free bed, and fell into a dreamless sleep.

SCRATCH-ch-ch-ch. SCRATCH-ch-ch-ch. SCRATCH-ch-ch-ch.

Massie ran her now-ragged, metallic-bronze manicured nails over the thigh of her slate gray Theory skirt. Deep red groves ran up and down her arms and legs, making them look like the World War I battlefields they were studying in class.

Plop!

A little folded-up paper triangle landed on Massie's desk like a raindrop on a cloudy day. She clenched her teeth and forced herself to look down. *Uch.* Not another one. Her friends had alternately been shooting her looks of pity about the kisstastrophe and giving her "helpful" bits of advice about the infestation.

She unfolded the lined notebook paper and recognized Dylan's messy blue scribble immediately: HAVE YOU TRIED A CHAMOMILE BATH? THAT WORKED WHEN I HAD THE POX.

A second later another note landed on her desk, this one written on graph paper in Alicia's slanty script: AT LEAST IT WASN'T SCORPIONS, LIKE THEY HAVE AT MY COUSIN NINA'S PLACE IN SPAIN. THEY PIIIIIIIINCH!

Before Massie even had a chance to turn around and give Alicia a look, her phone lit up with a text.

Kristen: When the people down the hall in my apt bldg had roaches, it only took a few days to fumigate.

Massie felt her face grow red. Was she hawnestly being compared to a tenant in Kristen's low-income apartment building? Especially one who was dirty enough to attract insects? What was the point of having money if it didn't protect you from natural disasters like this? Massie laid her burning forehead down on her cool oak desk.

"Massie." Mr. McGowan paused at the board. "Is everything okay?"

Massie sat back up and tried to make her face appear normal. "Uh-huh," she said. Her voice came out sounding more robotic than Wall-E's. *Beep-boop.*

"And so would you care to explain why the assassination of Archduke Ferdinand was the match that lit the powder keg of World War One?"

Massie wracked her brain for any shred of what he had just been talking about, but the only thing that was in there was a loop of images from the last eighteen hours: Landon's warm lips. His horrified face. His grandparents' shocked expressions on his Mac screen. The sight of the bugs crawling on her lavender Frette sheets.

Isaac had picked up Bean earlier that morning, and he'd returned home with a slice of birthday cake and a note from Landon that said, CALL ME. It was ahb-viously a pity note that Mrs. Crane had made him write.

"Um, no thank you," Massie said.

Mr. McGowan gave her a stern look. "Please pay more attention, Miss Block. I am not Alan Lambert and just 'Here for Your Entertainment.'"

Massie was so defeated, she didn't even have the energy to mention that his name was Adam, not Alan, and that she was *quite* aware Mr. McGowan was not placed on Earth for her amusement. The man was duller than a plastic spoon.

"Now, who can help Miss Block with the answer . . . ?"

Massie was hit with a wave of exhaustion so complete that she couldn't even work up the energy for a glare at Strawberry, who promptly answered the question. She was not only emotionally exhausted, but physically too. The night before, after finding that her bed had been turned into a jungle theme park, she'd moved into one of the guest rooms. But even there she hadn't felt safe from the bugs and their blood-sucking fangs and their multiple legs and their shiny, terrifying eyeballs. Eventually she'd tried to sleep in the bathtub of the guest bathroom, but it was hardly comfortable using porcelain for a pillow.

Finally, the bell rang.

Massie felt a pinch on her leg and instantly reached down—*SCRATCH-chchch. SCRATCH-chchch. SCRATCH-chchch*—before gathering her books.

"Ehma-it'sabouttime!" she said, sliding her chair back against the wood floor.

But the rest of the PC lagged behind. Dylan slowly stood up from her desk. Kristen was rooting through her leather messenger bag for something elusive. And Alicia pulled out a bottle of clear nail polish and started retouching her tips.

"Um, are you auditioning to be on RuPaul's new show?" Massie asked.

"No," her friends said in unison.

"Then why are you dragging?" She sighed dramatically. "Isaac's waiting."

Finally Alicia capped her nail polish and looked at Massie. "I'm sorry, Mass, but I read an article that said bedbugs can leap off someone's clothes and infect the person standing next to them."

"I have a really big indoor soccer game I can't miss," Kristen said, her eyes on the ground.

"Um, I need to walk more because of my new diet," Dylan said, chewing on the ends of her red hair, the way she always did when she was lying.

Massie stared at her friends. After an entire day of trying to hold it all together, she could feel her anger bubbling up inside her like a shaken bottle of Pellegrino. She closed her eyes and tried to picture the fluffy cloud, to put her bad feelings on it, to push it away. But the only clouds she could picture were those of a hurricane brewing on the horizon. She felt the low rumble of thunder rolling in. And the buzzing of lightning about to strike. The cold, angry rain pelting her shoulders. There was nothing she could do now. She was powerless to stop it.

But losing it at school brought a whole new meaning to LBR, so she just hitched her Coach bag higher on her shoulder and joined the out-of-school procession. Her boots clomped down the shiny wooden floor, ignoring the protests of the people she pushed out of her way. Through the open door at the end of the hall, she could see the familiar black shape of the Range Rover, the sun glinting off its windshield.

"Where are your friends?" Isaac asked when she opened the door, his brown eyes meeting Massie's in the rearview window.

"Let's just get out of here," Massie growled, popping her seatbelt into the buckle with a loud *click*. She slouched down in her seat, pretending to rub sidewalk salt off her boots, until she was out of view of the school. She did nawt need someone getting one hundred gossip points for spotting Massie Block driving home alone.

Fifteen minutes later, they pulled into the Blocks' driveway. Massie's phone started vibrating, and a picture of Landon holding Bark popped up on her screen. But she just sat there with the phone buzzing in her hand—because as shocked as she was to hear from her ex-crush, she was even more shocked at the appearance of her beloved home.

"Cirque de NO WAY!" Massie jumped out of the car.

It looked as though the circus had come to town and exploded all over the Block Estate. The entire mansion had been covered in an enormous, billowy red-and-blue tent. Her parents stood at the front of the house with fumigation masks on. At her father's feet was a set of matching, monogrammed Louis Vuitton suitcases. Her mother held Bean, who reached out a perfectly groomed paw toward Massie as she approached. At her mother's feet were Bean's matching, monogrammed Louis Vuitton puppy cases.

"What's going awn!?!" Massie screamed.

Her dad cleared his throat. "We're having the house fumigated."

Kendra adjusted her faux-fur chinchilla hat. "You can never be too careful when it comes to insect infestations." She reached out to tousle Massie's expertly tousled hair, but Massie pulled away. Kendra ended up grabbing at the air next to Massie's head instead.

"No one is allowed in the house until after the fumigation is finished," said William. "But look at it this way: It gives me and your mom the chance to finally get away on vacation to the Bahamas. And you get to bunk in the guesthouse with your pal Claire!"

Massie took two steps backward, feeling the storm clouds rolling in again. "I. Have. To. Live. With. Kuh-laire?" She dug her fingernails into her chapped, raw hands and narrowed her amber eyes. Suddenly she had a sneaking suspicion that she knew just where those bugs had come from.

"No need to thank us," Kendra said. "It will be like one big sleepover! We weren't able to get any of your clothes out, since your room was the site of the infestation. But I'm sure you can borrow things from Claire."

"THANK you?" Massie gasped.

"Well, okay." Kendra flashed her Chiclet-white smile. "You're welcome."

"Wh-wh-why can't I go on vacation with you?" Massie sputtered.

"Sorry, honey," her father said. "You have to stay in school."

A parade of official-looking men in protective rubber coats and gas masks marched down the flagstone path, holding clipboards and hoses and wearing bright orange backpacks with HAZMAT printed on the back.

Suddenly Kendra's iPhone started clucking like a chicken. "Oops, that's my alarm!" She leaned over and gave Massie a kiss on the cheek. "We have to get to the airport now, sweetheart!" Isaac loaded their suitcases into the Range Rover. "Really," Kendra said. "I know you're going to have a great week. Look at it as an adventure."

Her father gave Massie a hug, her mother placed Bean in Massie's arms, and then with the crunch of gravel beneath the Range Rover, they were off, leaving their daughter with nothing but her dog and the Michael Kors riding boots, high-waisted Theory pencil skirt, sleeveless silk blouse, and cashmere shrug on her back.

"Ready, set, GO!" Claire yelled into her computer's microphone, setting off a commotion of scissoring and taping. She, Cam, and Layne were having a contest over G-videochat to see who could wrap their holiday presents the fastest. Right then, Claire was using candy cane–print paper to speed-wrap a pair of robot walkie-talkies for Todd. Cam was covering a pair of fuzzy gray slippers for his father in gold foil. And Layne looked as if she were swimming in a sea of metallic blue Santa paper, wrapping a pair of bright pink Converse for herself—according to her, it was "the gift that kept on giving."

"Done!" cried Cam, holding his finished present in the air.

"Hey!" Layne said. "You cheated."

Claire giggled as she looked at Cam's "finished" present: a jagged sheet of gold was halfway wrapped around the slippers. A big piece of tape held the whole thing together.

"We never said it had to be wrapped *well*," Cam laughed, his green eye twinkling at her from the computer screen.

"True," said Claire as she stuck a shiny red bow on top of her neatly wrapped box.

"So what do I win?" he said.

"A bed full of bugs?" Layne said.

"I still can't believe you guys actually bugged Massie's room," Cam said, shaking his head.

Claire set out a new present—seashell earrings for her mom—on a sheet of Santas and prepared to cut around it.

"Shall I reenact the moment of discovery?" Layne said. Without waiting for his answer, she clutched her heart and threw herself onto her tie-dyed bedspread. "Argggggggggggggggghh! I've been infested with wildlife! Cover the house! Save my shoes!"

"I would have liked to see you in your bug-burglar outfit." Cam smiled at Claire.

She blushed. She was in crush with the way he supported her, even when she concocted crazy schemes like scaling a wall and breaking into her ex-bestie's house.

Layne interrupted her thoughts. "Status update," she said. "Get a room."

"I have a room," Claire said, motioning around her. "Unlike some people I know."

Cam coughed uncomfortably, and Claire looked up to see Massie standing in the doorway, hands on her Theory skirt–encased hips, tapping one nut-brown riding boot in slow motion.

Cam scratched his nose. Layne sneezed. Claire nibbled on her thumbnail. How did Massie manage to suck all the fun out of a room—or in this case, a video conference—like a high-powered Dirt Devil after a birthday party? She had to admit, though, that Massie wasn't looking good. She was barely a 3 today, while she usually hovered around a 9.2. Bags the size of silver dollars hung under her eyes, and her bare forearms had jagged red marks all over them, like she'd accidentally hugged a cactus. She had a soy stain on her cashmere shrug. And her usually pin-straight hair looked minutes away from kinking into a curl.

"Have you come to steal Christmas?" Layne said from the computer screen, curling a silver ribbon on the edge of her scissors blade like a butcher sharpening a carving knife.

Massie ignored Layne and blew her bangs out of her eyes. "Can anyone guess how this guesthouse is like my sense of style?"

"It's rigid and outdated?" Layne tried.

"No," Massie snarled. "It's MINE."

"Is everything okay, Massie?" Layne asked in a sugary-sweet voice. "It seems like you're *bugging* out."

"So are your eyes!" Massie said, scratching at the soy stain on her shrug.

Claire grimaced. Even Massie's comebacks had taken a dive. The alpha was in serious trouble. "I'm sorry you have to move out of your house," she said. "But you can borrow my PJs if you want. Rainbow gummies or reindeer print?"

Massie was quiet as she considered the two sets of flannel sleepwear—and perhaps Claire's act of kindness with them. But when she looked up, her face was devoid of any warmth, almost like she was the wax Madame Tussauds version of herself. "I would rather be fumigated than wear anything you own."

"She's just trying to be nice, Massie," said Cam, coming

to his crush's defense. His green eye was crinkled in outrage, but Claire could tell his blue eye was trying to maintain an air of reasonableness and sympathy.

"Well, that explains why she's hanging out with you," Massie snapped.

That did it! Massie could belittle Claire if she wanted, but Cam was off limits.

"Go to the spare room!" Claire ordered, her voice harder than a Jolly Rancher.

"Amen, sister!" Layne clapped from her bedroom.

Massie rolled her eyes, like she couldn't even be bothered to respond, then reached down and tore the candy-cane paper off Todd's walkie-talkies. With that, she whirled around and stomped out of the room, slamming the door behind her.

"Is it my imagination, or is she getting even meaner?" Cam asked.

"Is that even possible?" Layne affixed a mass of curly silver ribbon strands to her wax lips. "That would be like the ocean getting wetter."

Claire finished wrapping the earrings for her mom. This time last year, she'd bought a gold lion charm for Massie. The red metallic box it had come in was so pretty, she couldn't bring herself to wrap it. Massie had immediately put it on her charm bracelet and worn it every day since. Claire had always seen it as the moment they'd truly become friends. With a pang, she wondered if Massie had taken it off when she'd declared war on Claire.

Once again, just for a moment, Claire couldn't help but

feel guilty. Maybe she and Layne *had* gone too far. But no. Massie had brought this on herself by being controlling. She was a bully, and if this were the fifth sequel to *Bring it On*, this would be the part of the movie where Claire battled back from a bruised ankle (courtesy of Massie tripping her) only to rise to the top of the cheer-pyramid during the last seconds of the Nationals. She'd fist pump the air to the uber-emotional strains of Taylor Swift's "Fifteen," while Massie sat alone in the crowd, wearing an ill-fitting sports cap and eating a box of caramel popcorn.

And like that cheer-champion, Claire refused to feel bad. It was her turn to be on top.

"All the jingle ladies, all the jingle ladies," the Pretty Committee sang as they glided through the garlanded doors of the Westchester Mall.

Alicia and Kristen harmonized while Dylan swung her hips, narrowly avoiding knocking over a display of high heel–shaped gingerbread cookies near the Saks entrance. While her friends sang, Massie kept her Sugar-and-Spice Glossip Girl–glossed lips closed. She was on a mission.

And it did not involve caroling.

"Wow. They've literally decked the halls," Kristen said, admiring the Swarovski crystal lights that bordered every archway and window, and the red and green silk ribbons that draped artfully from ceiling to floor. Every store sparkled with tinsel and glass ornaments. The scent of pine filled the air. It was like walking through the most expensive forest in the world.

"Merry Christmas!" called an elf wearing curled green shoes, handing Massie a candy cane.

"Ugh," Massie growled. She cracked the candy in half and threw it back at the elf.

"Hey!" the elf cried, throwing up his hands to deflect the flying shards.

"The halls aren't the only things getting decked around here," Dylan joked, taking the candy cane another elf handed her and sticking it in her mouth.

"Point." Alicia lifted her finger. "What's wrong, Mass? Where's your holiday cheer?"

"Under a tent in my walk-in closet," Massie snapped. "Which is why we're here to buy me a new wardrobe."

She'd done the best she possibly could to transform yesterday's outfit: She'd hiked up her pencil skirt into a mini and tied two pink hair ribbons around her waist to give the illusion of a belt. Then she'd folded her ecru cashmere shrug into a rosette, which was now pinned to her sleeveless blouse. Sure, she looked great. But it was a recycled outfit, and while it may have been good for the environment, it was bad for the soul.

As they entered Saks, her phone buzzed with a text from Landon.

Landon: Did u get the cake?

She hit IGNORE. She couldn't even begin to think about Landon until she bought a new outfit. She pulled three index cards out of her purse and handed them to her friends. "Here are your shopping lists. Any questions?"

DYLAN—TOPS
COLORS
Acceptable: Wine, sapphire, bronze, gray (dark, not heather), eggplant, black, white, peach (but not too pink!), sage

Unacceptable: Emerald, powder pink, dusty lavender, yellow, puke green

FABRICS

Acceptable: Silk, tulle, linen, 100% cotton, sequins (bronze only).

Unacceptable: Anything with a greater than 5% blend. Rayon, polyester, mesh, netting. ABSOLUTELY NO LYCRA!

ALICIA—BOTTOMS (subset: Skirts)

STYLES

Acceptable: Mini, bubble, pockets (but not those big drapy ones that look like extra thighs).

Unacceptable: A-line, anything below $50, anything below the knee (makes even the skinniest calves look fat).

KRISTEN—BOTTOMS (subset: Pants and Shoes)

PANTS

Acceptable: Skinny, wide-leg, zippered bottoms, anklet, flared.

Unacceptable: Straight-leg, high-waisted, hip-ballooned, capri, pedal-pushers.

SHOES (SIZE: 6)

Acceptable: If you don't know by now what kind of shoes I like, then we have a problem.

Unacceptable: Starts with K and rhymes with dead.

Dylan cleared her throat as she scanned her list. "Um, Massie? Are you sure you don't want something with a little Lycra in it? It can be comfortable to stretch a little." She placed her hand on a Tory Burch boot and stretched her hammy.

Massie narrowed her eyes at the redhead. "No more bending! Also, sumptuous fabrics are in," she reminded her friends when they got to the contemporary designer section. "Think velvet and brocade." She held up a thin Theory crocheted sweater and placed it under a shrunken Elizabeth and James velvet blazer the color of her horse Brownie's mane. "You have fifteen minutes to browse. Text me the photos, avoid salespeople, and remember: NO LYCRA. Now, fan out!"

Dylan groaned, touching a black leather belt stitched with metallic silver thread. "I want to buy it all! Why did I spend my entire allowance?"

"Tell me about it," Alicia and Kristen said at the same time.

Massie caught sight of a kidney bean–shaped chaise longue by the dressing room. It was a perfect periwinkle velvet—a cross between Landon's eyes and a stormy ocean.

"Kristen," she barked. "Go ask the salesgirl if that chaise comes in a dress."

"But, Massie I don't think—" Kristen said slowly.

"Nike!" Massie snapped.

"How can I just do it if—"

"Nike!" Massie snapped again.

Kristen turned in a huff to find a salesgirl. Massie shooed the other girls away and started flipping through a rack of Rebecca Beeson dresses. Usually shopping with the PC was one of her favorite things to do, but today it brought her all the joy of an eyebrow wax. She pawed through silk skirt after shrunken blazer, feeling like a prisoner on death row. Only instead of picking her last meal, she had to pick her last outfit—the last outfit she would wear as Landon's crush.

By the time she'd worked her way through Laundry, BCBG, and Twelfth Street by Cynthia Vincent, Dylan, Alicia, and Kristen had returned, staggering under piles of jewel-toned fabrics.

"They don't have the couch in a dress," Kristen said, her pointy chin resting atop a pair of dark wash Citizens. "But they do have it in a pillow."

"Uch!" Massie stomped into the brightly lit dressing room and dropped her mound of clothes on a mushroom-shaped stool.

"Oof!" Dylan tripped over a fallen satin camisole. "Man down!"

"Gotcha!" Alicia dropped her armful of clothes to reach out and steady the redhead.

"A little privacy please," Massie snapped, shutting the doors against her friends. She turned to take in her booty—there were shirts, blazers, jeans, and shoes of every color and shape. She quickly pulled off her recycled outfit, instantly feeling lighter.

"Ahhhh!" she sighed happily as she tried on a draped, char-coal gray Alexander Wang jersey dress. The belted midsection showed off her waist, and the skirt stopped just above her knees, hiding the worst of her scratch-welts. The soft-as-Bean's-paws fabric soothed her itchy skin and reminded her of the true purpose of fashion: to make her look and feel great.

She came out of the dressing room with the strut of an alpha who'd never had to share a pillow with a cockroach or an intimate lip kiss with her ex-crush's grandparents. "Thoughts?"

Dylan, Kristen, and Alicia sat on the kidney bean. They all tilted their heads to the right.

"Beautiful."

"Classy yet fun."

"Ten!"

"Perfect." Massie went back inside and grabbed the outfit she'd discarded on the floor, throwing it in the dressing room's little metal trashcan with a satisfying *plunk*. "You know what?" she said over the door, pulling on a pair of black ribbed tights. "I'm just going to get all of it and try the rest on at home. Let's go get lattes. On me!"

Massie emerged from the dressing room still in the Alexander Wang dress, her arms laden with some of her best friends: Calvin, Dolce, and Marc, to name a few. As she led the PC to the counter, the lavender-and-steam scent of new clothing filled her nostrils, reminding her that some things—like her impeccable fashion sense and her ability to stay on top no matter the horrific circumstances—never change.

"Oh, I have this Alice + Olivia dress too. I love it," said the clerk as she rang everything up. Her name tag read SHELLY.

"Mmm," Massie sniffed. Then she handed over her Saks card and ripped the tags out of the military-style Elie Tahari jacket she'd placed over her new dress.

Dylan picked up a pair of silver polka-dotted socks hanging next to the counter. "I don't know how I feel about the whole socks-over-tights trend."

Alicia rolled her eyes. "That's because it's *not* a trend. It's a faux pas."

Shelly swiped Massie's silver card through her register. "Hm." Two dents like quotation marks formed between her brows. "I'm sorry, miss, but it's saying it's denied. Do you have another card you'd like to use?"

Massie sighed. "Here." She produced a Platinum AmEx. "Use this one instead."

The clerk slid it through, slowly and deliberately. A moment passed, then she spoke again. "Sorry, miss, but this one is denied too."

Alicia, Kristen, and Dylan fell silent. A line four-deep waited behind them.

"Maybe you're doing it wrong." Massie held her voice steady, but the word *denied* had sent 9.8-magnitude vibrations through her body. She handed over her Visa Black.

"Denied," said the clerk again. The quotation-mark wrinkles on her brow had smoothed out, but she didn't bother to hide the irritation in her voice.

"Try it again," Massie demanded. A Coach-clad mother and her wavy-haired teenage daughter joined the end of the line.

"I've tried it six ways to Sunday," said the clerk, as Coach Mom whispered, "What is that girl's problem?" to her daughter.

"This is why elementary school children shouldn't be allowed to shop alone," Wavy Hair replied with an exaggerated eye-roll.

"Well, try it to Monday, then," Massie insisted, resisting the urge to fan her pits with the card Shelly was trying to hand back to her.

Alicia tipped her head forward, her glossy black hair hiding her entire face. Dylan snapped on her sunglasses. Kristen traced a circle on the marble floor with her Puma-sneakered toe.

The clerk heaved a sigh but did as she was told. "Denied," she announced loudly.

"Shhhh!" Massie pawed through her purse for her last card; an emergency MasterCard in Bean's name. "I'm sure it's just because my parents are on vacation, and the credit card companies want to make sure nothing is being stolen," she said to the PC.

"That makes sense," Dylan said, though her voice sounded unnaturally high. "That happened to me once when Merri-Lee went to Fiji."

"Denied," the clerk singsonged, like Massie's credit card crisis was a musical number in an upcoming episode of *Glee*.

"This is ridiculous!" Massie pulled out her iPhone and dialed her mother's cell, just as the blond girl who Claire used to hang out with, the one from ADD—Carol? Cat? Cara?—joined the back of the line. A bead of sweat dropped from the back of Massie's hairline and trickled down her back. "You've reached Kendra Block . . ."

"It's Massie. Nine-one-one. Call me back." Massie hung up the phone.

"What are you going to do?" Kristen asked, picking at the hem of her Free People henley.

"Well, one of you will have to pay for these until I figure this mistake out."

Shelly made a *tsk-tsk* noise with her tongue. Two more people joined the line.

Gawd, thought Massie. Why was everyone and their mother shopping on a Thursday night?

"I spent all my allowance on my snow-day shopping spree." Dylan shrugged and took a few steps away from the counter.

"Remember?" Alicia shook her head. "I'm on 'browse' mode because of the promise I made to my parents. No shopping till January."

"Don't look at me," Kristen frowned. "I'm poor."

"Ehmagawd," Massie breathed. Then she redialed her mother with one hand and tossed her hair with the other.

"You've reached . . ."

Massie hung up and dialed again.

"You've reached . . ."

"WHY AREN'T YOU PICKING UP?" Massie yelled into the phone. "Call me." Redial.

"You've reached . . ."

"I know who I've reached!" Massie screamed.

"Echem." Shelly tapped her eggplant-polished nails on the granite countertop. "I'm going to need you to step aside so I can help these other costumers." She gestured to the line behind Massie, which had grown to nine customers.

Massie put her hands on the counter and leaned forward until she was just inches from Shelly's watery blue eyes. "Excuse me, but are you an iPhone on airplane mode?"

"No."

"Then RING ME UP."

Shelly placed a hand on the black phone in front of her. She picked it up and pressed a single red button. "Security," the clerk whispered. "We may have a situation."

Immediately, three guards clothed in gunmetal gray uniforms swarmed the counter.

"Miss, you'll need to come with us."

Massie felt like her entire body had been injected with Botox. She couldn't move, couldn't speak, couldn't open her mouth to form the flurry of angry words she wanted to hurl at the security guards. Instead, while the PC looked on, their hands clapped over their mouths, she just let the guards sweep her back to the dressing room, like they were the ocean and she was caught in a riptide.

One guard, a man with gray hair and crinkly green eyes, handed her the outfit she'd stuffed in the trash can.

"We're prepared to let you off with a warning," he said kindly, as though he were throwing her a life preserver. But all it did was remind her that she was drowning. And she had the sinking feeling that she hadn't even hit rock bottom.

After school on Friday—and following a sledding date with Cam—a snow-covered Claire pushed through her blue-painted front door, Layne at her heels.

The second she saw her living room, she stopped short.

Layne slammed into her back. "Woah, Nelly!" She grabbed Claire's shoulders to steady herself.

"Um, Massie?" Claire said, taking in the transformed state of her living room. "What's going on in here?"

Massie, wearing what looked like ripped silk boxers, stood in the center of the living room, sorting through a stack of DVDs. The lights were turned down low, and pillows from every room in the house—Claire's ORLAN-D'OH! Simpsons pillow, her parents' lacy shams, even Todd's old SpongeBob novelty pillow—were strewn around the coffee table. All of her mother's best candles were piled on the table next to a stack of old *Vogue*s. Bean was off to the side, snoozing on a pile of *Lucky*s.

Massie blinked in mock confusion. "What I do every Friday night. Host the PC's sleepover."

"Oh, I'm sorry." Claire blinked back, showing that she wasn't going to let Massie push her around. She crossed her arms and tilted her chin. "I forgot you had your weekly sleepovers in the living room of *my* house."

"Technically, it's *mine*," Massie answered, as if that explained everything.

"You're unbelievable," Claire muttered, gathering up the candles and putting them back in their boxes. Yes, technically the guesthouse belonged to the Blocks, but it was Claire's *home*. That had to count for something, didn't it?

Massie unpacked the candles again and placed a thick silver one on the table with a *bang*. "Wherever I am, the sleepover is. So, if I am forced to live in"—she looked around her, as if the room were a Salvation Army warehouse filled with coffee-stained furniture—"these conditions, this is where the sleepover will be." She picked up a bottle of Crabtree & Evelyn Clean Cotton Room Spray and spritzed madly, like she was a firing squad executing smelly prisoners.

"Do you even still have friends? Or have you Lycra'd them out of your life?" Claire said, sneezing as a waft of cotton smell settled over her.

"Good job!" Layne said, smacking Claire on the back.

"I guess you'll never know," Massie shrugged, ignoring Layne. "Because you're *nawt* invited."

"Like we care. Layne and I already have plans for tonight. And they don't involve lip-kissing our magazines." She motioned to an old copy of *Vanity Fair* with Robert Pattinson on the cover.

Layne pulled a bag of mini carrots from her pockets and nibbled on one like it was a piece of corn. "Wait, who has big plans? We do?"

"Yes," Claire said through gritted teeth. "Remember?"

"Oh. Right. Big plans." Layne turned to Massie and put her hands on her black jeans–clad hips. "Huge plans. We can't even talk about them because they're so top secret."

Massie rolled her eyes. "Well, I hope they don't involve makeovers of any kind. The world can't handle another follicle-challenged Lyons."

Claire gasped.

Layne bit off the top of a carrot.

"Watch out, Block," Claire snarled. "Karma's real. And what goes around, comes around."

Massie cocked a perfectly plucked brow. "Oh, you mean like my house getting infested with bugs?"

Claire blushed. Massie cocked her other brow as if to say *gotcha.*

But Layne just picked up one of the candles and held it above her head. "No, I mean you won't always be on top. What goes up, must come down." She dropped it on the floor, where it cracked in half.

Claire grinned. She loved how smart her best friend was. "It's a basic rule of gravity," she added.

Massie nudged the candle remains with her bare foot. Claire was surprised to note that the big toenail was chipped, indicating that Massie was at least three days past pedicure prime. "Kuh-laire and Layme, do I look like a bowl of egg whites?"

"No," Claire and Layne sighed in unison.

"Then why do you think you can beat me?" Massie said, picking up the candle pieces and crushing them in her hands.

"Just remember: Gravity doesn't work in reverse—two LBRs like you will never rise to the top."

Claire gasped. "Come on, Layne." She stomped toward the stairs. Whenever she thought Massie's meanness had reached its peak, the alpha would make another trek up Mean Everest.

As they reached the top step, Claire's phone buzzed—"Somebody" by Kings of Leon, Cam's signature ringtone. Four texts arrived, one after another:

Cam: Reading about Joan of Arc 4 history class.

Cam: Led French army by herself.

Cam: Reminds me of u.

The final text was a picture of Cam giving a thumbs-up sign to a page of his textbook. Under a photo of the French warrior girl decked out in her armor and shield, he'd stuck a little Post-it that read: CLAIRE OF ARC.

Claire smiled. Cam was a better ego boost than a thinning mirror. And his smile was like an eraser, wiping away the overwhelming sense of anger and helplessness she'd just felt. His green eye reminded her that she *was* powerful and strong, and his blue eye, which was narrowed in a half wink, told her she was just the girl to overthrow Massie's reign of bully-dom.

"That's it!" she declared as she and Layne reached her room. So what if Massie had more money and better comebacks? Claire had Layne and Cam and her mom and dad. She had a down-to-earth, affordable fashion sense and a new pair of lime green Keds that she had found ON SALE. And with those weapons at her disposal, she would usher in a new era of kindness and consideration, where it wasn't which designer name was on the sole of your shoes that mattered, but the actual quality of your soul.

Claire closed the door and booted up her iTunes. The room was instantly filled with the notes of a Snow Patrol song, the first track of the *Wintry Mix* CD that Cam had made her for Thanksgiving. After checking outside, she pulled the shades down on her windows.

"Are we being spied on?" Layne hissed, glancing around furtively. "Do we need disguises? I just bought a new edible mustache at Spencer's."

Claire shook her head and began pacing back and forth, holding her hands behind her back, like a general getting ready for battle. Or like Claire of Arc preparing to storm the fortress of snobbery.

"Layne!" she said, punching the air with her fist. "The current administration has had us under its thumb for too long."

"Obama?" Layne said. "But I like him."

"Think smaller, Layne."

Layne scratched her head with the carrot she'd just pulled out of her canvas bag. "Principal Burns?"

"Smaller," Claire sighed. "Think of the girl who is, as we speak, unrolling designer sleeping bags in my living room."

"Ah," Layne said. "Got it. The ole Blockade."

"Don't you think it's time for a change?"

"Down with the Massarchy!" Layne cried.

"No more head shavings of poor, defenseless little brothers. No more snide comments about affordable footwear. No more lice storms. No more efforts to control the hearts, minds, and crushes of the common eighth-grader," Claire said defiantly.

Layne jumped off the bed, pulled the light green shade from a lamp, putting on her head like a helmet, and began marching. "Let's Dolce their Gabbanas!"

Claire giggled. She had no idea what it meant, but she liked it. "Let's kick them in their Guccis!"

"Drop poos on their Choos!"

"And sneeze on their silk tees."

"And wham bam them in the L.A.M.B."

"But there's one more thing." Claire paused and clasped her hands over her heart, a stance she had seen on the text Cam had sent. "We need to get the message to the people."

"Done." Layne pulled out her iPhone. "I'll get Danh Bondak to help set up a rally, and I'll Facebook every girl I know."

Claire tapped her nose. "Perfect. But we'll need a slogan. No great campaign is successful without one."

"'Kindness: Melts your heart, not your hands'?" Layne suggested, still typing intently on her iPhone.

Claire tugged her bangs. "What about 'The Block stops here'?"

"Lacks pizzazz. Maybe something with *your* name." Layne screwed her face up, like a baby getting ready to take a poo. "I'VE GOT IT!" she shouted a second later. "'Dawn of a new Claire-a.' Get it? Claire-era, but pronounced *Clara*."

Claire clapped her hands. "Ohhh, I like it! You don't think it's too me-centric, though?"

"It's you-centric in a good way. You embody all the qualities of our cause: down-to-earth, nice, on a budget." Layne bent over Claire's computer and changed the song to "Defying Gravity," from the *Wicked* soundtrack.

Claire placed her hand on Layne's shoulder. "Layne, will you be my second in command?"

Layne frowned. "I have a pretty full schedule of wax-lip bracelet making, and cyber-stalking Art from the lizard store. What exactly would this position entail?"

Claire sat down at her desk and opened up a new document. The little black cursor blinked back at her. "We need a manifesto."

A squeal sounded from downstairs. Claire peeked out the window to see Alicia and Kristen waltzing in after Dylan. The scent of Angel wafted up the stairs, and Claire could hear air kisses down below.

"Sorry, we have to have the sleepover in this war zone . . ." Massie was shouting.

"Ohhh, SNAP!" Layne said.

"Commandment One!" Claire said, stabbing the keyboard with vigor. "Thou shalt put the 'end' in 'bad friend.'"

"Good one!" Layne said, sitting up on her heels. "Thou shalt not drink the last of the rice milk eggnog without buying a suitable replacement!"

Claire giggled. "Or spray smelly *parfum* in other peoples' houses."

"Or call you insulting names that sound similar to your name but aren't! Like *Layme*."

"Or shave someone's little brother bald!"

"Or mock your glue-gunning skillzzzz."

"Or think friendship bracelets are for people without friends."

"Or mock you for having an exotic palate."

Claire typed with Beth Orton–esque passion. An hour later their masterpiece was done:

THE DAWN OF A NEW CLAIRE-A

Thou shalt put the "end" in "bad friend."

Thou shalt not interfere with my friendships by spreading lice rumors or anything of the kind.

Thou shalt not say my name in vain.

Thou shalt uphold comfort over couture!

Thou shalt not think less of me for being middle-class.

Thou shalt not judge me on the amount of my allowance.

Thou shalt not tell me where I can sit at lunch. Freedom to graze must be granted.

Thou shalt not turn my friends against me during a fight.

Thou shalt not covet my crush.

Thou shalt not roll your eyes and talk about empty calories when sugar is being imbibed.

"Good work," said Claire, reading over the list. "Now, we should probably take an oath and promise to forever live by and uphold these ideals."

Layne held out her hand.

"Friends forever," Claire said.

"Enemies never," Layne said.

"No matter the weather," Claire said.

"Always together!" Layne said.

"No matter what you wear-a," Claire giggled.

"I will always . . . be . . . there-a?" Layne answered.

"We will live by these rules . . ."

"In and out of middle school!"

Claire could barely finish rhyming she was laughing so hard. "The dawn of a new . . ."

"Claire-a!" they finished together.

"Go, Mario, go!" Todd pumped one fist in the air as his Mario Kart racer shot across the finish line in first place. "Suck it, Bowser!" Todd jumped up. "Bald-head high-five!" He gave the side of his bald head a slap. The force of it knocked him backward, and he stumbled into the coffee table, knocking over the candles.

"Todd, will you PUH-LEASE turn that DOWN!" Massie yelled for the fourth time. "I am ON the PHONE!"

Actually she was on hold, listening to a jazzy instrumental version of "The Sun Will Come Out Tomorrow" as she had been for the last fifteen minutes, waiting to speak to a supervisor. She had, it seemed, spent the entire *day* on the phone, waiting for people's supervisors. And when she hadn't been on hold with the credit card companies, she was on hold with the assistants to the high-profile personal shoppers who were checking to see if their bosses would consider lending Massie some clothes until her parents got back. But all day long, no matter to whom she'd been talking, the answer had been the same: *Sorry, there's nothing we can do.*

The whole thing was more frustrating than conjugating irregular French verbs. Even the knowledge that her sleepover was about to begin didn't cheer her up at all. With her luck, it was bound to be a disaster.

Not only was Todd there, but the snacks were terrible. She couldn't order personal thin-crust whole-wheat pizzas with tropical fruit parfaits because of the credit debacle. Inez had the week off, and Judi Lyons's idea of gourmet was a basket of deflated Cheetos, a half-popped bag of microwave popcorn, and celery sticks with peanut butter and raisins (aka ants on a log, which, due to Massie's recent infestation, she did *nawt* appreciate).

The only possible bright spot was that she'd asked her friends to bring back all the clothes she'd lent them in the past year. There had to be *something* she could salvage. She was counting on it.

"Heck yeah!" Todd whooped.

"TODD!" Massie cried. "BE QUIET!"

"Owner's rights!" Todd called back, not taking his eyes off the screen.

"The Pretty Committee is getting here in ten minutes," she hissed.

Todd pressed PAUSE and turned to wink at Massie. "Don't worry. You don't need to be jealous of all the other babes." He turned back to the game. He and his virtual self crashed and screamed through virtual landscapes, and Massie was *thisclose* to nonvirtually killing him.

Bean wandered over, sniffed at a celery stick, and then lay back down. She was wearing one of her ah-dorable Prada parkas, but Massie could tell her pup's heart wasn't in it. She missed Bark Obama and snoozing on his doggy bed.

"I hear you, Bean," Massie said, rubbing under her pup's chin. "But this is our life now." She slumped down onto the blue-and-white-slipcovered couch and leaned her head on her fist, just as the hold-music feature started to replay the *Annie* soundtrack. She shook her head and finally hung up. Maybe she should try her parents again.

Suddenly her phone vibrated with a picture text. It was from Landon, and the picture was of Bark, who'd buried his nose in his paws and was looking at the camera with round, wet eyes.

She pressed IGNORE, and Bean shot her a disappointed look.

"I know, I know," Massie said. "But I can't let him see me like *this*." Massie motioned to her current outfit: she'd cut the arms off the shrug to make leg warmers and turned the pencil skirt into a tube top. She'd repurposed the blouse into a pair of silky, day-to-evening boxer shorts, which she wore over the same tights she'd been wearing since her parents had left the previous afternoon. She had gotten so desperate that she'd yanked a strand of translucent beads that Mrs. Lyons used as curtain tiebacks in the kitchen and tripled them to make a necklace. She didn't know whether she looked fabulous or was one fingerless glove away from looking like a runaway, but she had a whole new respect for the whiny contestants on *Project Runway*.

Furthermore, she had a blister on her thumb thanks to the stupid hot glue gun, and her hands were cramped from sewing, and the Lyonses' Febreze-scented living room was making her throat seize.

"I'm on FI-YAH!" Todd shouted, high-fiving his head again. The sudden sound broke Massie out of her reverie.

"You have fifteen more seconds, then I am unplugging that box," Massie yelled, getting ready to throw one of the couch cushions at him.

"So you can have me all to yourself?" Todd asked. "Don't worry, Princess Peach is no competition for you, baby."

"We're heeeeeeeeeeeeeeeeeeerrrrrreee," Dylan yelled, bursting into the living room.

"Finally!" Massie snapped as Alicia and Kristen filed in after her. Snowflakes dusted Alicia's long black lashes. The tip of Kristen's nose was pink from the cold.

The three of them dropped their sleeping bags, overnight bags, and suitcases (full of her old clothes, she hoped) on the floor.

Alicia eyed Massie's outfit and the glue gun on the coffee table. "Oh, are we having arts and crafts night?"

Massie self-consciously hugged the pillow to her chest, covering her outfit. For a brief moment, she remembered how it felt to be friends with her old crew, the Ahnnabees, who'd laughed at her for thinking charm bracelets were stylish.

Dylan picked up an ant on the log and sniffed it suspiciously before dropping it back on the plate. "It looks like poo-berries on a log!"

Kristen snorted.

"SCOOOOOOOORE!" Todd yelled.

Massie's skin sizzled. "THAT'S IT!" She crossed the room in five steps and unplugged the Wii.

"Heyyyyy! I was about to beat my fastest time!"

Mrs. Lyons, who was knitting in the kitchen, popped her head into the living room. "Todd, please let the girls have their sleepover. You can come help me make cookies if you want."

But Todd just glared at his mom and stormed up the stairs. Mrs. Lyons let out a loud sigh and retreated back into the kitchen.

Massie settled back onto the couch. Her friends were still eyeing the room warily, unsure of where they should sit. Massie's stomach knotted like one of the mini pretzels in the bowl Mrs. Lyons had put on the table.

"Luckily I raided a gift basket Brangelina sent my mom," Dylan said. From her leather hobo she pulled a cellophane clump filled with peppermint bark, dark chocolate pretzels, and salted caramels. She promptly dug in.

"I stopped at the magazine store," Alicia said, spreading out *US Weekly*, *People*, *Star*, and *Star UK*. She eyed the selection on the coffee table. "These ones are current. Don't worry. My treat."

Massie's cheeks burned. She turned her attention to the suitcases, dumping out the contents of Kristen's Adidas duffle, Dylan's LV trunk, and Alicia's Ralph wheelie. Neon yellow tube tops, slanted stripe sweaters, horseshoe-print blouses, high-waisted jeans, and satin camis tumbled out, rolling together like laundry on a spin cycle.

"Oh my gawd." Massie held up a slouchy-shouldered poof dress in lime green sateen. "This is so 1982!"

"Actually," Kristen corrected her. "It was 2009, when we all decided to dress like it was 1982."

Massie pulled out a pair of pointy-toed, knee-high boots while Kristen put on a pair of chunky gold hoop earrings.

"Look! I'm the ghost of Christmas Fashions Past," Dylan intoned in a low voice, draping a lavender pashmina over her head.

"And I'm Captain Jack Sparrow!" Kristen said, thrusting her arm through a ruffly white top.

"Point!" Alicia said, trying on a pair of square-toed Ferragamos.

"Gross," Massie said, holding up a pair of yoga pants. "I can't wear these. They're way too stretched out!"

Dylan paused, a big piece of peppermint bark halfway to her mouth. She sucked in her stomach. "Hey!"

"Ugh." Massie held up a beige sweater. "No wonder I lent this to you, Kristen. It works well on boxy, boyish figures."

"Excuse me!" Kristen squeezed her sides in an attempt to form an hourglass figure.

"Um, Leesh," Massie said, throwing the sweater onto her reject pile and picking up a Theory bra tee. "Why don't you look into a minimizer? Your boobs left saggy imprints in this shirt."

Kristen narrowed her eyes. Dylan pinched a piece of popcorn until it shattered.

Alicia crossed her arms over her C-cups. "If I wanted to be put through torture, I'd hit the Coach outlet on the Sunday before Christmas."

"Maybe you should, so you can stop borrowing my clothes and turning them into camel covers." Massie heard how mean the words were, and she registered the anger on her friends' faces. But it felt like she was a shaken can of Coke Zero—her anger tab had been popped open, and there was no stopping the spray of insults. "Dylan, if you're worried about the junk in your trunk, stop eating junk food. And Kristen, if you want to look like a girl, for Gawd's sake, get some highlights and *stop wearing sneakers*!"

"That's it." Alicia grabbed her magazines. "I'm out of here."

"Same!" Kristen shouted.

"Guys like my junk!" Dylan snarled, balling up the bag of popcorn in her hands.

As though watching an episode of *The Hills* where Audrina and Heidi have yet another falling out, Massie watched, oddly detached, as the three girls gathered up their things and marched through the door. A chill filled the room that had nothing to do with the temperature outside.

Claire's face peered around the edge of the steps. She was holding a clipboard and looking incredibly smug. Layne appeared behind her.

"Hear ye, hear ye!" Layne said. "All rise for the great and honorable Claire Lyons, who has a very important announcement."

"It's the dawn of a new Claire-a!" Claire said.

"A new what-a?" The end of Massie's nose felt numb. She reached up to touch it, to make sure it was still there. To check if this evening had actually happened—that it wasn't just some cheap candle smoke–induced hallucination. Faster than you could say *credit denied,* she had lost her crush, her house, and her wardrobe, and now her friends had abandoned her. She felt emptier than the foreclosed home down the street and more pathetic than Jessica Simpson's new reality show.

Layne rolled her eyes. "Claire-a. Like 'era.' Like a period of time. Only it sounds like Claire's name, so we're calling it Clai—"

Claire elbowed Layne. "Rule number one!" she shouted. "Thou shalt put the 'end' in 'bad friend.'"

"I'm going to put the 'up' in 'shut up,'" Massie said, pushing past Claire and bolting up the steps.

Claire darted after her, Layne close behind. "Rule number two: Thou shalt not interfere with my friendships by spreading lice rumors or anything of the kind."

"You are interfering with my patience right now, Kuh-lass-less." Massie reached the landing and turned around.

"Rule number three! Thou shalt not say my name in vain!" Claire yelled. "Rule number four!"

Massie ran into Claire's room, slammed the door behind her, and locked it.

"RULE NUMBER FIVE!" Claire shouted through the door.

Massie grabbed Claire's headphones, put them on, and turned up the volume. *Wicked*'s "Defying Gravity" blasted into her ears.

"Let me in!" Claire pounded on the door. "This is my room!"

"Open up!" Layne yelled.

With a shaking hand, Massie turned the volume even louder, understanding for the first time why LBRs hide in the world of virtual reality.

The door shook. Claire and Layne faded into the background and the lyrics took over.

IT'S TIME TO TRY
DEFYING GRAVITY
I THINK I'LL TRY
DEFYING GRAVITY
AND YOU CAN'T PULL ME DOWN!

Once the pounding stopped, Massie whipped off the headphones. She hadn't defied gravity. She'd sunken to its lowest depths.

"I can't believe people actually came," Claire whispered to Layne and Cam. "Are you sure they're really all here for us? Or did a new *Twilight* book come out today? A scratch-and-sniff version maybe? In 3–D?"

Layne grinned. "This is for us, Claire. It's all YOU. And after all, we did Facebook everyone from OCD *and* Briarwood. The people are ready for this. POWER TO THE LITTLE PEOPLE!" she shouted.

All the people within earshot broke into cheers. She turned back to Claire. "See? I'm going to go hand out more flyers." She motioned to a stack of hot-pink A NEW CLAIRE-A WILL GET YOU THERE-A flyers and then disappeared into the crowd.

It was the first official rally of the new Claire-a, and despite the cold, a small but rabid crowd of about twenty-five people had gathered outside Forbidden Planet. They were talking, laughing, dancing in place, using their asthma inhalers, putting wax on their braces, and Tweeting the event, all to the pumping strains of Jay-Z's "Off That," which, thanks to Danh, could be heard for blocks. Kori, Meena, Strawberry, and Heather marched through, holding two giant banners Layne had given them. One read USHER IN A NEW CLAIRE-A (complete with a Photoshopped picture of Usher and Claire, giving each

139

other a high five), and on the other they'd put IT'S THE DAWN OF A NEW CLAIRE-A in orange, pink, yellow, and red—or, as Layne put it, "dawn colors."

To Massie it probably would have looked like a gathering for a makeover show "before." But to Claire it looked like an assembly of future world leaders: smart, fun, creative people who had been persecuted by the current regime. Well, no more!

Danh approached and tapped his tiny laptop. "All systems are go on our end," he said.

On the minuscule screen of his laptop, Claire could see the members of OCD's astronomy club, their backs to an enormous window on Westchester Hill. They all gave Claire a thumbs-up, and she gave a thumbs-up right back.

Claire walked back up to the stage, which had been assembled by the OCD stage crew—what Massie would have called "theater geeks"—and stood behind the podium. She scanned the parking lot, her heart hammering in her chest. Off to one side a group of theater buffs (who had asked her four times if headshots would be required for the rally) were practicing an a cappella version of "One Day More" from *Les Misérables* as per Layne's request.

Cam and Layne approached the podium. Layne wore a whistle around her neck.

"How you doing there, slugger? You're looking a little scared-a," said Layne.

Claire bit her lip. "I'm nervous," she said. "I don't like public speaking. What if they don't like what I have to say?"

Cam massaged her shoulders like she was a prizefighter and he was the coach. "We've got this in the bag," he said. "All you have to do is lay out the rules of the Claire-a, and they will love it."

Layne wrapped a towel around her shoulders and squirted a quick shot of Smartwater into Claire's mouth. "Listen, kid," she said. "You've got big dreams, and now is the time to make them real. I want you to go out there and knock 'em dead. Do it for Milton and Bernice."

"Who are Milton and Bernice?" Claire said.

"They're my grandparents. They were both shy kids. Anyway, those people out there? They want to hear those rules; they *need* to hear those rules. So get out there and show these peeps what you got!"

With that, Layne pushed Claire on stage, toward the microphone Danh had set up.

Claire adjusted the mic, which made a shrill squeal. The audience groaned. She looked out over the crowd. Kori and Strawberry leaned forward. The choir kids belted their puffy coats and blew on their hands. Danh fiddled with his laptop.

"Well, now that I have your attention . . ." Claire laughed nervously. In the awkward silence that followed, Claire wracked her brain for the first line of the speech she and Layne had prepared. Something about justice—no, people. Something about justice and people.

"L . . . B . . . R . . ." Layne mouthed frantically from stage left. Cam gave her a thumbs-up, and Claire felt a thrill run through her.

Right. LBRs.

She stood up straight as a prima ballerina and shouted, "How many of you have been called an LBR? How many have had to endure eye-rolls at your outfits?" Several hands in the audience went up. "Or been asked to move from where you were sitting at lunch to make room for someone's purse?" In her periphery, she could see Layne raise her hand. Claire raised her own.

"Massie asked me to move lockers because she didn't like how my grape-scented erasers smelled," one girl yelled.

"She asked me if I was related to Picasso because my left boob is bigger than my right one!"

"She asked me if my cell was E.T.'s, cuz I only use it to phone home!" Olivia Ryan called out.

Claire shook her head. "How many of you have been mocked for liking theater, art, computers, chess, astronomy, medical textbooks . . . ?"

More hands went up. People were shouting out their grievances.

"She told me chess was for people who didn't have chests!"

"She said all painters go crazy from the fumes!"

"She said theater is for geeks who want to *act* like they're cool."

Still more hands.

Claire looked sternly out over the crowd. "And how many of you are ready for a time when you can pursue the hobbies you want to pursue, with no worry of extracurricular persecution at your school?"

Now, all the hands in the audience were raised. Claire smiled. She leaned into the microphone.

"Well then, it's time for . . . " Her heart was pounding. She looked over at Cam and Layne, who were nodding and pumping their fists. "It's time for"—she took a breath—"THE DAWN OF A NEW CLAIRE-A!"

At first the crowd was silent. Claire's throat went dry. But then Danh started clapping. Then a girl next to him joined in. More and more people were clapping, until suddenly, the entire group erupted with the sounds of high fives and cheers. Danh held up his laptop, and Claire could see the members of the astronomy club jumping up and down.

Claire felt Layne's elbow nudge hers. She opened her mouth for another shot of Smartwater.

"Doin' good, boss," Layne said. "They're loving it. And you haven't even gotten to the list of the rules yet!"

Claire took a deep breath and started again. "And so, it is in the spirit of change that I present to you the ten rules, the ten commandments of our cause! Number one: Thou shalt put the END in bad FRIEND!"

A loud *whoop!* came from the crowd.

"Number two . . ." Claire continued.

Behind her, Strawberry, Kori, Meena, and Heather were at the ready with ten poster boards, each printed with one of the commandments. As Claire read them out, the girls paraded behind her, holding their signs up high.

The reading of each additional commandment was met with shouts and cheers, murmurs of approval, and fists thrown high in the air. More than once Claire had to stop and wait for everyone to quiet down. By the time she got to the last one, she was hoarse from shouting.

"And number ten: Thou shalt not roll your eyes and talk about empty calories when we are EATING DELICIOUS PROCESSED SUGAR TREATS!"

And as she said *treats*, Layne reached into an enormous Sweetsations sack and pulled out handfuls of individually wrapped gummies: planets, protractors, paintbrushes, sea creatures, and gummy words printed in Latin. She tossed them into the crowd.

"But what will we do if Massie and the PC come back against us in full force?" shouted Carol, the head of the art club.

"We will stay calm and strong and rational. We will stay together so that none of us has to encounter bullying alone," Claire said.

Layne led a chorus of *woo-hoo*s.

"Can I list this as an extracurricular activity for college applications?" asked Meredith, a member of the P.P.C.C. (the Pre-Pre-College Club).

"Sure," Claire said. "Why not?" She formed her left hand into a *C* shape and held it up. "This *C* is for *Claire-a*," she shouted. Then with her right arm she made a muscle. "This is for strength!" Then she flashed a peace sign with her left hand and held it up. "And this is a peace sign for the tone of our philosophy." She did the whole thing again in one fluid movement. The crowd *ooh*ed. "This will be our signal," she said. "So that we can recognize one another out in the field, recruit new members, and give one another strength!"

Claire watched as everyone in the crowd tried it. "Now go forth," she finished. "Live by these ideals and mottos. Together, we can bring a new era to OCD, to Briarwood, and to the world!"

And with that, Layne turned up Jay-Z's "Off That" again, and everyone started to cheer, holding their hands up in *C*s and peace signs.

"Social persecution!" Claire yelled.

"We're off that!" screamed the crowd, punching the air.

"Getting made fun of for our fashion choices!" she yelled.

"We're off that!"

In a fit of jubilant excitement, the theater group busted into "One Day More." Claire stepped off the stage. Her entire body buzzed with energy. She could barely get through the crowd for all the people reaching out to shake her hand, pump her shoulders, and pat her on the back. A girl came up and handed Claire a tiny puppy and then snapped a picture. "For her Facebook page," she explained, pointing to the puppy.

"This has been a long time coming!" another girl said. "I'm going to write an essay for *The Octavian Courier*."

"Massie and the PC won't know what hit them!"

"I hope I can get school credit for this!"

"Viva la Claire!"

Cam gave her a big hug, and Claire's heart was filled with the warm s'mores feeling she got whenever she was near him.

Layne got the audio guys to turn the music up. And then she started marching out. Claire walked next to her. The rest of the crowd followed, shouting, "Claire-a, Claire-a, Claire-a!"

It seemed as though power was finally going to the people—just where it had always belonged.

Massie kicked Claire's festive candy-cane sheets to the floor, along with her green-and-red elf-covered comforter, and sat up in bed. If there was one thing worse than going to sleep in a bed full of bugs, it was waking up in a coarse tangle of jolly holiday sheets. At least with bugs you *expected* to be itchy.

"Beeeeean," Massie moaned. "Please make it Sunday again."

Usually by Monday morning, Massie felt refreshed from a weekend of sleepovers, shopping, and seeing her crush du jour. But this weekend had contained none of those things, and Massie felt more worn than her poor pencil skirt.

She'd tossed and turned all night in Claire's scratchy sheets, which were even less comfortable than the ones in the Block house's guest room, trying to escape the haunting images of Landon's grandparents discussing the "fast young lady" who'd smooched their grandson on the Internet. Or her friends walking out on her, one by one. Or declined credit cards, swiping with ease for someone else while other shoppers laughed, as she had to make do with her one bedraggled outfit. With each turn, she'd chafed her legs and rubbed her elbows rawer than yellowtail sushi.

And just when she'd finally drifted off, Claire had started banging on the door, demanding to be let in. Then Mrs. Lyons had knocked and called her name through the door. But Massie had pretended to be asleep. And she wished she were still asleep now. Because through the window she could see her still-tented house, meaning she had to face yet another day as a crushless, outfitless, and possibly friendless outcast.

Her phone buzzed with an e-mail.

TO: Massie
FROM: Mom and Dad
SUBJECT: Hi hi!

Hello, darling.

You and Claire must be having a great time! It's bright and sunny every day here. We got you and Bean matching leis! The boat is so lovely. How fun would it be to live on one for a year?

We'll be home tomorrow.

Air kisses!
Mom & Dad

PS: We tried calling last night. Judy said you were out cold. Must be all the fun you and Claire are having!

Thank Gawd! Her parents were coming home tomorrow. The thought filled her with some hope—but not much. Because she still had to get through today in her outfit. Like those shipwreck survivors who survived on mangos and then could never eat them again, Massie planned to renounce Theory as soon as this nightmare was over.

"Come on, Bean," Massie groaned. "Time to go meet the enemy. Or have breakfast with it . . . or whatever."

Massie put on her Dolce & Gabbana sunglasses (the Lyonses' blinds were highly ineffective) and went to the chair where she was sure she'd thrown her outfit last night. It wasn't there. "Maybe it's under the covers," she told Bean, throwing Claire's scratchy terry cloth robe over her night-gown, aka the stretched-out-boob shirt she'd lent Alicia. She padded down the hallway to the stairs. When she reached the bottom landing, the smell of turkey bacon tickled her nostrils and the sound of laughter hit her ears.

"Can you believe it?" Mr. Lyons roared. "A sourdough pretzel!"

"More like a sour-*grape* pretzel," Mrs. Lyons joked.

Weird. The Blocks never talked in the morning. Massie's father was usually already at work by the time Massie left for school, and her mother had early tennis lessons with Andre, a tennis pro whose biceps were so big that he had to get his ten-nis shirts custom-tailored. Massie normally just grabbed a Luna bar from the cabinet and hopped into the Range Rover to go to school.

"There you are!" Mrs. Lyons jumped up from the square, white wooden table when Massie entered the kitchen. She lay a cool hand on Massie's forehead. "I was so worried when you slept through my knocking."

Claire choked on her poppy-seed bagel. Todd pounded her on the back.

"Oh, I had earplugs in," Massie lied, glaring at Claire. "Todd's newts have been keeping me up."

"I can't help it if my newts are nocturnal," Todd said.

"Say that ten times fast," Judi laughed.

What was *with* these people? It wasn't even eight a.m., and they were acting like they were on *Regis and Kelly*. Massie winced under her sunglasses and tried to just focus on her main objectives: finding her clothes, which had gone MIA, and figuring out how to turn them into a dress using only dental floss and a stapler.

Massie poured herself a glass of orange juice from the Minute Maid carton. "Judi, did you know this is only fifteen percent juice? And you should really buy calcium fortified. It would help Claire's nails grow more normally."

Claire jumped up from her stool and stormed upstairs. A minute later, Massie heard the sound of a door slamming.

Judi sighed wearily as Massie put some kibble in a bowl for Bean. The dog gave it a hesitant sniff. "I'm sorry, Bean," she whispered, "but they don't have au jus in this house."

"Massie, sweetie, what kind of eggs do you want?" Mrs. Lyons asked, standing up.

Massie shrugged.

"Well, then it'll just have to be a surprise!"

Mrs. Lyons wandered off, and Massie sat down at the table next to Todd. He was staring at her. She poured a bowl of cereal and (*ugh!*) whole milk. When she looked up, he was still staring at her.

"*WHAT?!*" Massie spat.

"You look like a spy in those glasses," Todd said.

"You look like a cherry Tootsie Pop," Massie replied.

Judi shot Massie a *be nice* frown.

"I thought you liked my baldness."

"I bet you believe Santa Claus is real too," Massie scoffed.

"What?" Todd swung around to face his mom, then turned back to Massie, his pointy jaw slack. From the kitchen, Judi made a slashing movement across her throat.

"Sorry." Massie shrugged. "I thought he knew."

Todd's jaw dropped and his eyes went wide, like he'd been mortally wounded. When Mrs. Lyons came back into the room with a plate of eggs sunny-side up, Todd skulked out, mumbling an excuse about having to get ready for school.

Mrs. Lyons had a worried expression on her face.

"He had to find out some time. Have you seen my clothes?" Massie asked, ignoring the Santa drama. "They've gone missing."

Mrs. Lyons frowned. "You've worn them for four days straight. I put them in the wash."

"What?" Massie's elbow slipped off the table in shock. "But they're the only clothes I have!"

"Try Claire's closet," Mrs. Lyons said, hurrying after her son.

Wear Claire's clothes!? Massie could feel a lifetime of

alphaness unraveling like a sweater from Forever 21. But maybe, just maybe, there would be something of her own in Claire's closet. She had given Claire hand-me-downs at times over the last year—maybe there was *something* salvageable.

The door to Claire's bedroom was open. Her lemon-yellow CD locker stood at the far wall, and a now-worn sheepskin carpet was at the foot of the bed. Her Simpsons ORLAN-D'OH! pillow was on the floor. Massie stood in front of the closet and steeled herself.

She opened the silver-handled door and gasped.

It was emptier than Barney's after the end-of-season sale. In fact, there were only two things hanging in there. A pair of OshKoshB'gosh overalls—the very same pair Claire had worn when she'd arrived in Westchester—and a very wrinkly powder pink T-shirt.

She had hidden *everything,* even her ironic Sesame Street tee. If Massie had still been friends with Claire, she'd have given twenty gossip points for this move.

But now . . .

"KUH-LAIRE!"

But the only response was a car door slamming. Massie ran to the window to see Mr. Lyonses' beige Ford Taurus, with Claire in the front passenger seat, reversing out of the driveway. Exhaust billowed from the tailpipe like a poltergeist in the frigid air.

"She had to leave early," Mrs. Lyons called, from downstairs. "Some school project."

Massie stared at the overalls and the T-shirt. There was only one option now.

Massie clutched her stomach. "Judi!" she yelled, barely faking the agony in her voice. "I think I ate some bad sushi!"

Then she wrapped herself up in the rough sheets like a giant loser hand roll and stuck her tongue out at the elves. They seemed to be laughing at her.

"Kuh-laire," Layne said in her best Massie voice as she sur-veyed the scene from the entrance to the New Green Café. Three eighth-graders walked by in slouchy blue, red, and green sweatpants. "Did I *authorize* a sweatpants parade?"

The girls flashed the *C* peace sign as they passed.

Claire giggled and led Layne to a table in the middle of the café. Even though she'd gotten almost no sleep the night before—Todd's newts had clawed around in the gravel all night—she felt like she'd downed an entire case of 5-Hour Energy.

She knew her rally had been a success, but she also knew there was a big difference between what people would say in a parking lot and what they'd actually do when they got back inside the walls of OCD. But a lot of girls had chosen comfort over couture today, making Claire happier than when she was getting a whiff of Cam's Drakkar Noir. It was the make-under of the century: At least thirty girls had put on sweatpants, stuffed their athletic-socked feet in fUggs, and traded in their contacts for chunky glasses.

But of all the changes at OCD today, the most surprising one was what had happened to Table 18. Since the beginning of time, or at least since before Claire moved to Westchester,

Table 18 had belonged to Massie and the PC. No one else would even dare walk too close to it, let alone try to sit there.

But today, on a cold Monday in December, Kori, Strawberry, Heather, and Meena had joined Claire and Layne at the table.

"And then we took the ostrich eggs and turned them into lamps," Kori said. She was telling a story about visiting her grandmother's ostrich farm in Texas.

"Will you pass the paisley paper?" Meena asked Heather, who passed her a stack of yellow and blue paper. The girls were folding hundreds of small, silky pieces of paper into cranes. Kori had told Claire that cranes were meant to bring a sick person good health, and the girls were planning to send them to a sick child in Westchester whom they had read about in the newspaper.

"Claire-a!" A seventh-grade girl in an extra-large I ♥ NEW YORK T-shirt fist-bumped Claire and Layne as she walked by, her tray piled high with crème brulee *and* French fries.

"This might be the best day ever," Claire declared as she finished a metallic red crane. Her toes were comfortable in her gray-and-baby-blue Skechers. She felt loose and un-Lycra'd in her zip-up hoodie. And her cheeks hurt from the grin that had been plastered on her face since she'd arrived at school and seen Meena and Heather in hemp pants.

"One of the lunch ladies told me they can't keep up with the dessert orders!" Layne said, slurping down her avocado smoothie.

"The rice pudding is amazing!" Olivia exclaimed, eating a large spoonful.

Claire's smile broadened even further. She reached up and pushed her cheeks toward her lips. If she wasn't careful, she'd end up looking like the Joker.

A girl named Nancy Sims stopped by the table. "Layne, if I live near Five Corners, which bus should I take?"

Layne pulled out her clipboard. "The W24."

"Thanks!" Nancy said, flashing a *C* before skipping off.

"Nicely done!" Claire high-fived her friend.

Layne tipped her clipboard toward Claire. "I have fifty 'I'm on a Bus' signatures." In honor of the new Claire-a, Layne had launched an "Eco over Ego" campaign to reduce OCD's carbon footprint. She wanted to revamp the whole bus experience by promising to provide top-100 mixes to be played during the ride; she was going to petition the school board to map out newly planned bus routes that would take them past the boys' school. "A lot of the girls said they were going to take public transportation on the weekends, too, so their parents won't have to drive as much. And Danh Bondak told me he's going to see if the country club will rent out golf carts to underage drivers, to promote electric cars."

Becca Wilder and Rachel Walker approached, wearing matching OCD sweatshirts.

"OMG, Claire, you've changed my life!" Becca gushed. "I've been pretending to not understand algebra all year, because Massie once said that algebras are for algeboobs and who needs math when you have an iPhone. But this morning, I finally admitted that I'm a math genius. I aced my exam!"

"THANK YOU!" Rachel exclaimed, her auburn hair flying forward as she took Claire by the shoulders. She stuck a foot in the air—on it was a bright purple bunny slipper. "Thank you for making it safe to wear comfortable shoes for the first time in my entire life. Alicia said I looked like a deranged school mascot, but I didn't even care!"

"No problem," Claire said, waving her own sneakers at Rachel. "Happy to help."

BAM!

The sound of a door banging open and hitting the wall cut through the air, and the entire café went silent.

"Uh-oh." Layne pointed. "Here comes trouble."

In the doorway stood Kristen, Dylan, and Alicia, looking as stunned as Taylor Swift during the 2009 VMAs when Kanye stole her acceptance speech. Kristen put her hands on her skinny-jeaned hips. Alicia crossed her arms over her C-cups.

"Chaaaaaaaaaaaaaaaaaaaaaos," Dylan burped, tugging on the ends of her red hair.

"I think . . . I may faint," Alicia said, breathing into a paper bag.

Kristen reached out a hand to steady her friend. "It's okay," she said. "We're obviously dreaming. In a second we'll wake up and everything will be back to normal."

"I don't think this is a dream," Dylan said, gawking at the trays of two girls walking past, laden with French fries and chocolate cheesecake.

One by one, the girls took out their phones and started

dialing, no doubt sending an SOS to Massie, who—as Claire had expected—was a no-show. She was probably still standing in front of the closet, staring at the lone pair of overalls. In retrospect, Claire felt a teeny bit bad about leaving her ex-friend nothing to wear. But this was war, and Massie had stolen her room first.

Alicia's knees started to buckle, and she grabbed onto Kristen for support. "Look," she yelled, pointing at Kori and the cranes. "There are LBRs at our table."

Kristen's mouth fell open. Dylan gasped.

Layne let out a little giggle. "I'm so glad they started selling chocolate-covered popcorn, because I'm going to need it to watch this show."

The three girls crossed to what had always been their table with the caution of a bunch of lab-coated scientists approaching a family of gorillas. When they got to Table 18, it took Alicia several *echem*s before anyone took notice of them.

"Oh, hello!" Strawberry said brightly, when she finally looked up from folding a crane. "How are you?"

"Um," Alicia said, her voice cracking. "I'm going to have to have Rosette, my cleaning woman, come disinfect this table. If you get up right now, I won't bill you for the case of Lysol."

The girls at the table looked at one another. Claire widened her eyes at Layne, telling her telepathically to give the others a chance to stand up for themselves first.

Then Kori said, "Well, we're already making great headway into our crane project, and we can't really move everything now. Why don't you join in and help?"

"Yes," Claire agreed, motioning to an empty chair. "Come sit."

"I don't want to make a bunch of weird birds out of garbage," Alicia said, ignoring Claire.

"They're not weird birds," Kori explained. "They're paper cranes."

"Well, maybe some of your little cranes can lift you up and fly you somewhere else. This is our table, and you're sitting at it," Alicia said. Her hands were on her hips and her glossed lips were pursed.

"There's plenty of room, why don't you just sit with us?" Strawberry said. A few of the girls moved their things to make room for the PC.

"We could show you how to make them," Meena said. "And you could have some of my sweet potato fries."

Dylan started to reach out to take a couple, but Alicia smacked her hand away. "We don't sit with losers," she hissed.

"Yeah, we sit *on* them," said Dylan, managing to snag a fry.

A moment passed.

"You're going to sit on us?" Strawberry bit her lip, clearly trying not to laugh.

"Ouch," said Kori. "That would probably hurt."

Dylan whipped the fry at Kori.

Kori took out a spray bottle.

Claire's stomach clenched. She leaped up. "NOT YET!" she shouted.

But it was too late. Kori spritzed it at Dylan's soft pink fingernails.

"What the . . . ?" Dylan jumped back. She looked down at her nails and sniffed. "Nail polish remover?" She dropped to the floor and dumped out her purse, searching through a collection of Essie, Chanel, and OPI nail polish containers.

Kristen's gaze bounced like a bobblehead between Table 18 and Dylan.

"Help me!" Dylan cried. After a beat, Kristen knelt down in her BDG skinnys and shifted through Dylan's possessions, until she held up the powder pink one that matched her friend's rapidly deteriorating manicure.

"Hey!" Kori and Strawberry yelled in unison.

Claire watched, speechless, as Alicia lifted Kori and Strawberry's wooden food trays off the table and dumped them in the trash. She shot them an *I dare you to retaliate* glare. The entire cafeteria felt silent, watching the spectacle at Table 18 like it was the season finale of *American Idol*.

As if triggered by some silent cue, Kori, Strawberry, Meena, Heather, and Olivia pulled vials of Jovan Musk out of their handbags.

"Three . . . two . . . one!" Strawberry shouted.

Alicia's mouth parted in horror as a cloud of musk enveloped her white cashmere sweater. She immediately started hacking.

"My eyes!" Dylan shrieked, shutting her eyes and groping to put her polish back in her bag.

"My nostrils!" Kristen yelled.

"Retreat!" Alicia shoved Dylan and Kristen toward the exit. The three girls ran out of the cafeteria, pulling out their cells as they went.

The entire café exploded into applause. And just like that, every single girl in the cafeteria, even the ones still wearing uncomfortable heels and constricting jeans, rushed Table 18.

"Wow," Layne whispered. "This must have been what our parents felt like when they watched the moon landing."

"I know." Claire had never thought she would see the day either. But Kori and the girls had stood their ground.

Layne scrambled onto her chair and took a bow.

Claire applauded along with the others, her pulse skipping through her veins. She couldn't believe what she'd started.

"Hey, Claire of Arc," Layne looked down from her chair. "Are you going to join me? You did start this entire movement, after all."

After another quick glance around for Principal Burns or a teacher, Claire threw caution to the wind and climbed on top of her chair. She made a *C,* then a muscle, then a peace sign.

"Claire-a, Claire-a," chanted the girls.

"Take back LBR!" yelled Layne. "Let's Be Real!"

"Let's Be Real!" answered the girls. "Let's Be Real! Let's Be Real!"

"Let's Be Real!" Claire yelled along with them. Sally

Richards put on her glasses, Allie Rose smiled through her braces. And Kori—aka "The Croissant" because of her curved posture—stood up straight for the very first time.

Claire was on top of the world. Or at least on top of OCD—right where she was determined to stay.

Alone at the Lyonses' house, Massie flipped through the channels on their small-screen TV and wondered how anyone could live with a television this tiny. "How do they even read the captions on *The Hills* on Telemundo?" she asked Bean.

Bean whimpered in response.

"I know you need a walk, but I can't go outside like *this*." Massie pulled the Lyonses' burnt-orange, handmade afghan around the overalls she'd been forced to wear. She prayed that whatever lived inside the stinky old yarn was asleep.

She checked her phone for the 137th time and sighed. No new texts. Yes, she'd Lycra-ed her friends out of the sleepover, but still. Why weren't they worried about her? Why weren't they sending her e-cards or ginseng smoothies?

On *All My Children*, a well-dressed older woman was plotting to gain control of a multimillion-dollar company. She enlisted the help of a sidekick whose idea of high fashion was gold lamé stockings with Converse sneakers. Massie grimaced. What these people needed were makeovers, not company takeovers.

Click.

A family sitcom came on that Massie had never seen. The

163

oldest son was apparently obsessed with a girl from school whom the rest of the family hated. She had long blond hair that she kept in a perfectly maintained ponytail, and she traipsed around school telling people why they were in or out of style. *She seems ah-mazing,* Massie thought. But then a boy with dark curly hair and bluer-than-blue eyes came on screen, reminding her of Landon. Her heart constricted like a too-tight bra.

Click.

On a local station, a news reporter with thick eyebrows was interviewing people at the Westchester Mall. Apparently, the mall was suffering record-breaking lulls in sales.

Probably because they keep declining my credit card!

Click.

She felt her eyes fill with tears and threw down the remote.

Bean looked up. She had refused to sleep in, on, or around any of the Lyonses' afghans or blankets, so she was perched awkwardly on the white coffee table.

"Poor thing," Massie said. "You must be freezing."

Bean whimpered and reached her paw for the door. But Massie just took the dog in her lap and petted her, trying to think of what she should do next. It was a free day, after all. Maybe she could go through Claire's makeup and give herself a manicure and pedicure. Through the window, she could see the exterminators starting to dismantle the striped canvas tent. Thank Gawd. If Massie had to live at the Lyons' one more day, she'd go crazier than Lindsay after a run-in with the paparazzi.

Her phone exploded with incoming texts.

"Ehmagheddon!" Massie shrieked. She looked down at her texts and read them one after another, a smile spreading across her face. Her friends missed her!

Dylan: Sorry we fought . . . School n-sane!
Alicia: Forgive & forget? Got sprayed with Jovan Musk.
I smell like cus!
Kristen: Sorry 'bout r fight. LBRs R sitting @ 18!

"Woof!"

"I'm sorry Bean, you will just have to hold it," Massie said distractedly. She could feel her malaise lifting like teased hair. Her friends needed her—just like always. Mini rebellion aside, they recognized her as their forever-alpha.

Then her phone buzzed with a new message from Dylan: a video of Claire and Layne standing on a table in the middle of the New Green Café, pumping their fists and jumping up and down. All around them, LBRs were doing some sort of weird arm and hand signals, like a bunch of queerleaders.

Then, the audio clicked in and Massie heard what they were chanting: LET'S BE REAL!

LET'S BE REAL! LET'S BE REAL! LET'S BE REAL!

Massie's emotions swirled like a Pucci scarf. This was unheard of—and the opposite of acceptable. LBRs at

Table 18? Claire and Layne on a table, chanting ridiculous things that didn't even rhyme? Totally unfashionable people trying to take over the school? One absence, and her empire crumbled. She opened a group text to all her friends.

Massie: How could you let this happen?

No one responded. Massie rolled her eyes and sighed. This was no time to push her friends away. If anything, she needed them more than ever. Massie texted again.

Massie: Claire is bread in the oven: about to be toast!

Her phone immediately pinged.

Kristen: ☺
Dylan: ☺ ☺
Alicia: Point!!! ☺

Massie felt a sudden burst of energy—something that felt almost like happiness. Let Claire enjoy her little coup now. Let her and Layne think running a school was as easy as scooping raisins onto their Cheerios. Let them hop up and down in their Keds. When Massie's house was bug-free and she was reunited with her wardrobe, she would remind these losers what LBR *really* stood for.

Bean let out a long, high-pitched whimper.

She sighed. "Okay, okay. Come on. But we're only going to the end of the driveway!"

Throwing the afghan over the overalls, Massie grabbed Bean's leash and walked to the front. The second she opened it, though, Bean was overcome by her own burst of energy. She ran forward, barking loudly, tugging Massie forward, down the driveway and around the corner.

"Bean!" Massie said. "Slow down!"

But Bean wouldn't listen. It was warmer today than it had been recently, but a cold wind bit at Massie's cheeks and her feet slipped over the icy sidewalk.

"Slow down!" They whizzed past the Keatings' Spanish-style mansion, then tore through the Vanderwoudes' snowy front yard. The afghan caught on the spindly branch of a barren crab apple tree—and stayed there. All Massie could do was look back as it hung forlornly from the branch like an orange ghost.

Cars honked, and a blue-outfitted USPS worker laughed at her. But still Bean didn't slow down. Massie's lungs burned and her eyes watered as she sprinted after her puppy, down Mayfair Street, then around another corner . . . where she led Massie straight into the leash of another dog.

She followed the leash up to a strong hand, a navy cashmere coat–covered arm, a broad shoulder, a perfect jaw, a high cheekbone—and finally she found herself staring into Caribbean blue eyes. Her heart immediately started hammering.

"Landon?"

He looked down at the ground. "Hey." His voice was as cold as the icy air blowing past them.

A red Jetta drove by, and a light turned on inside the white colonial home next to them.

Massie looked over to see Bean squatting on a dead flower bed as she peed . . . and peed . . . and peed. Each squirt extinguished a little piece of Massie's will to live. But finally Bean stood up and jumped on Bark, who *yip*-laughed and squirmed away. Bark then jumped on Bean, who howled with happiness.

Landon let out a great, loud, sputtering cough. Massie's face burned from shame. Of all the people on Earth she could have run into at that very moment in her OshKoshB-*kill-me-now* Claire-iffic getup . . . It probably looked like she'd escaped from preschool. She wanted to crawl behind a fire hydrant and hide, but the only thing lamer than wearing a bad outfit was running away in shame.

Landon finished coughing and turned back to stare at her. "I thought the fresh air would make me feel better, but now I'm not so sure."

Oh Gawd. The sight of Massie in her baggy denim ensemble was making him sick. It was probably bad fashion–induced anaphylactic shock, or worse—death by eyesore.

Landon wiped his nose with a tissue. "Sick day."

Even though it was snotty, Massie was jealous of the tissue. She wanted to be that close to him. "Oh," she said. "Right."

Massie looked at him more closely. He was as ah-dorable

as ever, of course, but his usual healthy glow *was* slightly dimmer. His nose was red and his forehead looked pale, and there were dark, mascara-smudge-looking circles under his eyes. For a moment, she was overtaken with the urge to follow Landon home, tuck him into bed, and order him some tomato soup with grilled Parmesan croutons.

But then she remembered that he was about to dump her, and she quickly shook off the Florence Nightingale fantasy.

"So why are you home today?" Landon said.

"Working on a project," she lied, straightening her shoulders.

Landon looked at her overalls.

She thumbed a denim suspender. "It's, um, part of the project—a psychological experiment to see if people act differently when they're wearing embarrassing outfits."

Landon's eyes narrowed. He made a motion like he was going to speak, but then he stopped himself.

Bean tugged at her leash, rolling over and over with Bark. Massie braced herself as Landon shuffled his feet a little, trying not to notice the adorable pair of Pumas he was wearing. "Well, good luck with that experiment." He turned to leave, but didn't move.

"Wait!"

Landon raised his thick eyebrows in a *yeah what is it* sort of way. Massie had no idea what to do next. She had never been so lost for words. Crushing on a ninth-grader was terrifying. All she could do was feel underdressed, underglossed, and underworded.

Landon finally looked up and stared Massie straight in the eye. Her heart pounded even harder. "Look. I know video-chatting with my grandparents isn't all that cool," he said. "But . . ." He straightened himself to his full height so he was towering over her. Massie felt like she was going to faint, right there, in a pile of three-day-old slush and outdated denim. "They're pretty cool for old people. So if you want to ditch me over it, fine. But just tell me instead of ignoring my texts."

Massie felt like she had just been run over by a crowd of screaming girls at a Jonas Brothers concert. *Landon* was embarrassed? This whole time she had been agonizing over her clothes, over the apoca-lips, over the fact that he was on the verge of dumping her. But the entire time he'd been agonizing too, not over how to break up with her, but over whether she thought he was an LBR for liking his grandparents?

A frenzy of barks and sniffs erupted beside them.

"Hey." Landon smiled. "Easy there, boy."

"Bean!" Massie called out.

But Bean kept chasing Bark, and then Bark started chasing Bean around the front yard of the white colonial. They started running circles around each other as if it were May Day and Landon and Massie were the maypole.

"Bean, stop!" Massie cried as the leash wound around her legs.

"Bark!" Landon said at the same time, as his own puppy figure-eighted around his legs.

Suddenly Bean and Barked jerked in opposite directions,

pulling Massie and Landon together. She felt like she was in a romantic comedy—without the comedy part.

"Oh no!" Massie said as she started to wobble. Landon swayed too, and all of a sudden she found herself an eyelash distance away from Landon's lashes. Could he smell her Glossip Girl Minted Rose lip gloss? And from this close, she could see his eyes weren't just Caribbean blue. There were also flecks of yellow, green, and brown—like glitter nail polish.

"I think it's ah-dorable that you talk to your grandparents all the time," she said, quietly. "I wish I was closer to my grandparents."

"You do?" Landon's voice was almost a whisper. He blushed. Massie thought it made him even cuter.

She nodded. "I was just embarrassed that they saw us kiss. And I thought you were probably embarrassed too."

Landon scrunched up his nose. "If I was embarrassed, why would I keep texting you?"

She traced a crack in the sidewalk with her toe. "I dunno. Maybe I was embarrassed. It's never happened before, so I didn't know what it felt like. And I didn't call you back because I thought you were going to . . . that you didn't . . ." She blushed. When she looked at him, he was looking right at her. And he was shaking his head, slow and sweet, in a way that made her know that she didn't even need to finish her sentence.

Their eyes met, and neither of them looked away this time.

Landon smiled. "Don't worry. No one's watching."

Eh.

My.

Gawd!

Landon leaned in. She could smell his cologne. It was something spicy and fresh. But at that moment, she couldn't even think of the name.

Massie let her eyelids fall closed like a light dimmer, and a moment later she felt his lips on hers. They were soft, and she let herself lean into him a little more.

He pulled away. "I shouldn't do this."

Massie's teeth chattered in a way that had nothing to do with the December air. *Not again!* "Why?" *What did I do wrong?* she wanted to shout.

Landon coughed. "I don't want to get you sick."

"Good point." Faking sick was one thing, but actually *being* sick was a pretty-buster.

"Yeah," he said, smiling back. "I guess it is."

They stood for a moment, looking at each other and smiling. Bark and Bean had calmed down and were cuddled up in yin-and-yang formation on the icy pavement.

Landon gathered Bark's leash in his hand, getting ready to walk away. "I'd better get back to the house. My mom only let me walk around on the condition that I wouldn't be out long. But I want to say before I go: You look really . . ." He hesitated.

Massie closed her eyes. *Silly? Unfashionable? Lumpy. Weird. Unmoisturized—*

". . . cute in those overalls."

A warm feeling spread throughout Massie's limbs in spite of the cold as Landon and Bark waved goodbye. Turning to go, she hooked her thumbs through her belt loops, thinking perhaps it was time to bring overalls back into vogue. If anyone could, it was Massie.

And then, just like overalls, Massie was back—and better than ever.

Claire and Layne stood by Claire's locker in the middle of the after-school rush.

"I just can't believe this is the same school we were in just *yesterday*," Claire said, shaking her head sadly as Rachel Walker teetered past in four-inch stiletto boots, pain evident on her face. The day before, OCD had felt like it was under a magical spell. But by Tuesday afternoon, the comfort-over-couture movement seemed like a dry marker–induced hallucination. "How could things have changed so fast?"

But Claire didn't need to wait for an answer, because she was looking right at it and its name was Massie Block.

"Take that!" Becca Wilder was pointing her Jovan Musk at the alpha. But Massie—hands covered by yellow latex gloves—just pulled out a mini fan as Becca spritzed, sending the musky cloud right back in Becca's face. Kristen, Alicia, and Dylan cheered Massie on, high-fiving one another in their own sets of rubber gloves.

"Arg-ul-Jovan!" Becca gurgled, her cheeks turning bright red.

"Repeat after me," Massie said coolly. "Alg-ge-*boob*."

Becca's sweatshirt-covered shoulders sagged like Kirstie Alley's couch. "Algeboob," she mumbled.

174

Each syllable was like a baseball bat to Claire's heart. It had been like this all day. Massie had reappeared at OCD that morning, wearing a pair of overalls so gorgeous that people were walking into lockers while gaping at them. They'd been such a hit, she'd started taking orders for custom-made "Massie-alls" since first period.

In theory, Claire knew the overalls had to be the ones she'd left in her closet, although looking at them now, that just didn't seem possible. The old ones had been a shapeless sack. But these were perfectly fitted to each leg and dyed a deep indigo. The straps were black silk ribbon tied into bows on both of her shoulders, contrasting perfectly with the deconstructed ivory tank she wore underneath. The outfit was both tough and sweet, just like a jawbreaker—and just like Massie.

In a few short hours, the alpha had managed to turn almost everything back to the way it had been before the supposed dawn of a new Claire-a. Massie had fanned away every Jovan spray, held out a gloved hand to every nail polish remover spritz attack, mocked every mock turtleneck, and scoffed at every pair of sweats until almost every girl had changed her outfit or simply gone home for the rest of the day.

"I just really thought the Claire-a would have some staying power," Claire said, sticking her math book on the top shelf of her locker.

"Was Joan of Arc such a defeatist?" Layne asked pointedly, adjusting her lens-less, square black glasses.

Across the hall, Massie let out a delicate little sneeze. Becca quickly took a packet of tissues out of her sweatshirt pocket and handed them to her. In lieu of *thank you,* Massie just said, "Now, should I put you down for a pair of Massie-alls?" Becca nodded before walking away, muttering something about her GPA taking a dive.

Behind Massie, the members of the PC smiled and nodded too. Yesterday they'd looked miserable, annoyed, and downright *scared*. But at the moment they looked more unflappable than Teflon. And maybe Claire was imagining it, but it seemed like the PC (latex gloves aside) were dressed even more stylishly than usual, perhaps to counteract the day of clothes freedom. Alicia wore head-to-toe Ralph along with gold drop earrings and a peacock feather headband. Dylan's sapphire blue tank dress fit her like a glove. And Kristen's hair shone in the sunlight.

"Good job!" Layne yelled irritably as Massie let out another delicate sneeze.

Massie's eyes flicked over Layne's elastic-waisted maternity jeans (*The better for eating hot dogs in,* she'd told Claire) and camo Crocs. "Sorry, I can't say the same. *Achooo!*"

Layne rolled her eyes and turned back to Claire. "What's with all the sneezing?" Maybe it wasn't just about the Jovan Musk cloud hanging in the hallway.

Claire shut her locker door with a bang. According to the rumor mill, Massie and Landon had shared a super-romantic, dog-leash-involved lip kiss the day before. Apparently he was sick, and now she was wearing her cold like some girls wear their crushes' sweaters. Kori had overheard Massie tell Alicia in math class that she "never knew H1N1 could be so romantic!"

Weird as it was, after all that had happened between them, some little part of Claire was sad to be missing out on this. If they were still on good terms, Claire would have been the first to know. She and Massie would have lounged on Claire's bed, drinking Smartwater and writing fake wedding announcements.

And now not only weren't they friends, Massie wasn't even bothering to be mean to her anymore. She was just acting like Claire wasn't there at all. Like she was a useless little bug who'd already been tented and exterminated.

Claire sighed.

"Buck up," said Layne. "More French fries for us. We still have a few converts, anyway." She pointed to a clump of seventh-grade girls in sweats standing near the exit. Their unmade-up eyes were growing wide with fear as Massie made her way over to them.

"Not for long," Claire pointed out.

Massie and the rest of the PC made their way toward the exit, gossiping and giggling just like usual. They were all looking at something on Massie's phone.

Anger washed over Claire, from the roots of her blond hair down to the tips of her lime green Keds. Her revolution was fading faster than a fake tan, right before her eyes.

But as the sweats-wearing seventh-graders put in special orders for overalls, the anger turned into a tidal wave of sadness. Not because the Sweat Girls were choosing Massie . . . but because Claire couldn't.

No matter how many bugs they put in Massie's bed, or whether she'd had a truly humiliating lip kiss, or was kicked out of her house or separated from all her possessions, Massie had the ability to rise from the ashes, to take a pair of over-used, gross denims and turn them into something beautiful.

And it was inspiring.

As soon as she reached OCD's double doors, Massie air-kissed her friends good bye so she wouldn't give them Landon's cold. It was microscopic, DNA-level proof that she'd finally conquered her fear of lip-kissing an older guy. And it was all hers. She'd sneeze every day of her life if it meant getting to kiss her crush.

She got into the Range Rover. Ordinarily Isaac would have given them all rides to their own houses, or they'd be coming to Massie's, but not today. Today was special.

"Issac, do you think it's possible to wear every single thing I own all at once?" Massie asked.

Issac shook his head. "I think it's possible to try."

Staring out the tinted window, Massie happily replayed the events of the past day and a half in her head—starting with the kiss, followed by a designer session with Inez, who'd promised to help her mass-produce her overalls, and a full eight hours of LBR re-education.

She'd managed to reclaim the school by first period, an impressive feat, even for an alpha. Her mind pulled up an image of Claire and Layne huddled by their lockers, Claire's light blue eyes looking as dull as the mashed potatoes the new café had served. Her shoulders had been slumped, and her boyfriend jeans had an ink stain on them.

Massie had never seen Claire look so defeated. Unstylish, yes, but Massie had always (secretly) admired her former friend's resilience. She'd done what no other girl at OCD had: gone from LBR to Pretty Committee. And if Massie was being hawnest, Claire was the only person who'd ever successfully stood up to her.

Massie's stomach flipped. It felt a lot like sadness. But maybe it was just a reaction to the seaweed salad she'd eaten at lunch.

A few minutes later, Issac turned onto Massie's road and pulled up the crashed gravel, semi-circular driveway.

"Ehma-amazing!!!"

It felt like the heavens had opened and Gawd herself was smiling down on Massie and her home. Gone was the red-and-blue tent around her beautiful stone estate. It was the first time she'd seen her house in days. The stately columns glowed pure white in the early afternoon sun. The gleaming windows winked their hellos. And the flagstone front path was snow-free—and more important, fumigation truck free.

The crazy circus had finally ended. She was home. Finally.

She skipped into the living room, where her parents were waiting on the white linen couch.

"Thank Gawd you're back!" Massie said. "You won't believe what I had to endure while you were gone. I couldn't use any of my credit cards! They were all declined. Can we sue?" Massie expected their jaws to drop in horror and shame for what they'd put her through. She expected a barrage of apologies and promises to give her the black diamond bangles from her Christmas list early, just to make up for it. But her parents just stared at her. And not in a good way.

Her mom's amber eyes were red. And she could have sworn her dad had at least three more gray hairs than when he'd left.

"You don't look tan," Massie said, suddenly. "Why don't you look tan? Or rested?"

Kendra shot her husband a worried look.

He clenched his square jaw. "Do you want to start?" he said quietly to his wife.

"Why don't you go, dear?" Kendra whispered back.

William pulled up his black Armani pant leg and crossed his legs. Then he rolled up the cuff of his green pinstriped button-down. Massie recognized the motions. He'd gone through the same routine that summer when he'd fired their gardener for forgetting to put the sprinklers on timer. "We have something to tell you, Massie," he said.

Kendra patted the cushion on the couch next to her. "Maybe you should sit down."

Massie felt the hairs stand up on the back of her neck. "Ehmgawd," she said, scratching a sudden itch that had popped up on her leg. "Did you find more bugs?"

Her mom let out a fake, high-pitched laugh, the one she used on William's business partners when they tried to be funny but weren't.

"We lied to you," Kendra said.

"Lied?" Massie echoed. Her tongue felt thick.

"We weren't really in the Bahamas. We were at the Hamptons house, getting it ready for sale."

SALE?

"What?" Massie grabbed the cushion below her like it was a floatation device and she was in the middle of an emergency landing. "But you love that house!" The Blocks spent every summer there. Her mother had gone through four different designers to make sure every last crystal sconce and eighteenth-century-style molding was correct.

"The market has taken a dip," Kendra said. Her forehead creased with concern. Massie had never seen Kendra's forehead move at all, let alone crease.

Massie's heart started hammering in her chest. "Are you going to buy a different house, then? A smaller one?"

"No," William said simply.

Kendra reached out and patted Massie's hand. "Everyone's lost money recently, honey. It's affected the whole world."

Massie's entire body felt cold. She stared at her father. "Like, how much money?" Her own voice sounded hollow, even to her own ears.

Her father smiled at Massie, but his eyebrows crinkled the way they did when he was worried. The room was completely silent.

Suddenly, there came a crazy, high-pitched, dog whistle–toned scream. Massie reached her hands up to plug her ears. And then she realized that she was the one screaming. She slapped her hand over her mouth and forced herself to swallow her scream. It settled into a hard ball in her stomach.

They were kidding. Of course they were kidding. They had to be kidding. This was some sort of elaborate ruse they'd concocted on the plane back to New York. A little *welcome home* joke before they presented their beloved daughter with her own brand-new yacht. She just had to calm down.

Fire breath in . . .

Fire breath out . . .

Fire breath in . . .

Fire breath out . . .

Fire breath out . . .

"Well, then," Kendra said finally. She cleared her throat. "We're going to have to make a few changes around here."

"Wait. Wait a second. You're serious?" Massie said.

Kendra nodded.

"Like, we're not going to be able to put the tennis courts in this summer? What about Andre? Will he give you lessons only twice a week now?" Massie felt a small, carat-sized tear wobble in the corner of her eye.

Kendra pressed her lips together. "I'm not really that into tennis right now."

"Not into tennis?" Massie screamed. "Am I going to have to wait to get my new Louis Vuitton bags? And what about my allowance?"

Kendra said, "Well, not right now . . ."

"Little changes will go a long way," her father said, trying to sound cheerful. "We'll bounce back. Eventually . . ."

Massie's breath came in short, rapid bursts. Her heart panged dangerously, and she could almost swear there was a tingling in her left arm. *Is this what it feels like to have a heart attack?* "When is 'eventually'?" she managed to ask.

"We don't know that just yet," Kendra said. But the way she said it gave Massie the sinking feeling that her mom *did* know. Or at least she had some idea. But she wasn't telling.

Which meant it was even worse than Massie thought.

Massie sank down to the floor as the reality of what they were saying sank in. She pulled her knees to her chest, with no regard for how much it was wrinkling her Massie-alls. She stared at the plush carpet in shock. One by one a parade of horrible questions marched into her brain: Would the carpet have to go? Would Inez? Then another, horrible thought hit her. Would *Isaac* have to go? And what would she tell Landon? And, ehmagawd, what would she tell the PC? How could she be their alpha if she couldn't even afford a latte at Starbucks?

"Listen, sweetie." Kendra knelt down so she was face-to-face with Massie. "We will overcome this." She squeezed Massie's hand and tried to smile. But she couldn't quite do it.

With that, the one-carat tear that had been wobbling in Massie's eye finally worked its way down her cheek. Massie could see it glittering out of the corner of her eye. It was followed by another—and another.

Massie realized it was probably the only sparkle she'd see this Christmas.

"You doing okay, honey?" Judi Lyons asked, patting Claire on the shoulder. "It's a lot to take in."

Claire nodded, stunned by what her parents had just told her. One minute she'd been G-chatting online with Cam, and the next minute her parents had come into her room with these looks on their faces and said the Blocks were having financial trouble. They were about to go through a very hard time. Big changes were coming.

"Chin up, kiddo. We're Lyonses," Jay Lyons said, pushing himself off Claire's bed. "And what do Lyons do?"

"We roar," Claire mumbled, hugging her stuffed giraffe to her chest.

"That's right," Mr. Lyons nodded.

"We're going to be okay, Claire Bear, I promise." Her mom kissed her on the forehead, then shuffled out of the room behind her husband.

But it wasn't *her* family Claire was worried about.

It was Massie.

Suddenly it felt like the past month was nothing but an ugly drawing on an Etch A Sketch that her parents had just shaken, erasing all the hurt and anger and fighting. All that remained was the fact that Massie's life was about to change.

This was about more than head shaving or clothing or where people sat in the cafeteria. It was about the fact that Massie would be devastated.

In a certain way, money wasn't all that important. Claire knew that. But having your worst nightmare come true was. So Claire did what you do when a friend is in trouble: She put aside her petty grievances and decided to try and cheer up Massie.

Grabbing a bag of gummies off her desk and the *Gossip Girl* DVD set out of her CD locker, she put on her coat, told her parents she'd be back soon, and padded slowly across the icy lawn.

Inside the Block mansion, things were surprisingly still and calm. The plush rugs were still plush, and the freshly waxed floors were still freshly waxed. The display of orchids still emitted their subtle exotic scent from the marble mail table. But even though it all looked the same, Claire knew that everything had changed.

She walked up the stairs. A thin sliver of cool light escaped from under Massie's door. "Massie?" she called, softly.

There was no answer.

"Massie?" Claire called again.

Still no answer.

After a minute of waiting and a quick bang swipe, Claire pushed the door open slowly and tiptoed inside.

Massie was on her bed, beneath her down duvet, hugging piles of clothes. She was crying softly, her legs making a tent around Bean, who had her nose buried in her paws.

"It's me. I heard," Claire said.

The lump on the bed didn't move, but Massie's tear-soaked voice rose from the pile of down. "What do you want?"

"I wanted to see if you were okay." Claire walked over to the bed and put her hand on Massie's knee.

Massie didn't move from her pretzel pose. "I'm doing just great. Ah-bviously."

"I'm so, so sorry Massie." Claire sat gently on the side of the bed. "I'm so, so sorry that this happened to you and your family. It really totally and completely sucks. It just does. But you guys are going to be okay, I know that. And the bright side is that you don't need money to be happy. I mean, look at me and my family. We don't have a lot of money, but we're happy. Your family will be just like that."

Massie sniffled, but she didn't look up.

"I brought you this," Claire held up her bag. "It's *Gossip Girl* season two. And . . ." She pulled a small bag of gummies out of her pocket. "Gummy crabs from my emergency stash."

"You brought these . . . for me?" Massie sat up a little, wiping her mascara-stained cheeks.

"The gummies, yeah. The DVD I found under the couch," Claire admitted. "You must have left it there at some point."

Massie finally looked up. Her amber eyes met Claire's cornflower blue ones.

And just like that, Claire felt like they were looking past the weeks of petty fights and stupid pranks, looking past everything they'd been through, and just really *looking* at each other. And finally each seeing, in the other, what had been there all along: someone to talk to, someone to laugh with, a confidante, a neighbor, a friend.

Claire smiled. Any moment now, Massie would rise up and throw herself tearfully into Claire's arms, admitting that Claire was the closest friend she'd ever had and the only person she could ever be herself around.

Claire would give Massie tips on how to be middle-class. Soon, they'd shop the sale sections together, look for Elie Tahari and BCBGirl at T.J. Maxx, and wear outfits more than once. And Massie would finally learn about the comfort and cuteness that was Nanette Lepore for Keds.

Massie blinked and smiled slightly.

Claire opened her arms for the hug she knew was coming.

"Go away."

Claire winced and stepped back. Her cheeks burned, as though Massie had just slapped her.

Massie propped herself up on her pillows. "When I want advice, I will watch Dr. Phil." Her cheeks were bright red, and not from MAC shimmer powder. "And the rumor isn't true, so don't go spreading it. And don't come here to gloat. Now puh-lease take your peace offerings, make like autumn, and *leaf*."

With that, Massie threw herself back down on the bed and buried her head in her arms. Claire sat stunned for a moment. She opened and closed her mouth a few times, but no words would come out.

Finally, she stood up, feeling as though she were moving

underwater. The *Gossip Girl* case slid off her lap and landed on the floor. DVDs spun out everywhere. Disc 1 hit the wall and cracked in two.

Claire knew exactly how it felt.

Massie stood just outside the bathroom door of the pizza shop as the scent of garlic, oregano, and melted cheese curled out to meet her. Normally, the promise of a piece of Slice of Heaven's organic, low-fat tofurkey Sicilian made her stomach grumble and her mouth water, but right then it made Massie feel sicker than really bad sushi.

The sloping walls of Slice of Heaven—the shop was built in the shape of a pizza oven—felt like they were caving in on Massie. She watched her friends elbow one another and dive into a giant deep-dish pizza, laughing like it was any regular day. And for them, it was. She didn't know how criminals on the run or people who'd had secret plastic surgery did it. Just a few hours of keeping her family's secret, and she was ready to explode. How had Kristen done it for so long?

Somehow, though, she had managed to get through the entire school day without crying in class or blurting out that she was poor. Not that it had been easy. All day long she'd felt like a breast implant about to burst. She had intentionally avoided making eye contact with all her friends. And three times she'd had to run to the bathroom for a stall-bawl. (Well, twice to cry, once to reapply her mascara.) She didn't know how she could possibly get through an evening with the people who knew her best in the world. The people she used to have so much in common with.

She watched as Dylan threw back her professionally straightened hair—$1,500 a pop—as she laughed. Alicia pushed her Prada sunglasses—$375—up on her head. Kristen adjusted her rose gold Tiffany heart-key drop necklace—a $410 birthday gift from Massie.

Her friends had so much luxury in their lives. Well, not Kristen, maybe. But were Alicia and Dylan aware at all of how much privilege they had? Did they even appreciate it? Their lives were so carefree—they could buy anything they wanted, and they had no idea how lucky they were.

From now on, the only things Massie would have of value were her friends. But that, she had to admit, was priceless.

And a-one, a-two, a-one, two, three . . . Massie straightened her spine and gave herself a silent countdown. On four, she forced herself to reenter the dining area with all the confidence of regular old pre-poverty Massie.

Only no one had told the six-year-old running around the pizza parlor that Massie was trying to make an entrance. He ran straight into her, knocking her into a busboy, who dropped the four empty pizza tins he was carrying with an ear-shattering *CLANG*. The PC and their ninth-grade crushes looked up and laughed.

"Party foul!"

"Man down!"

Massie did her best to regain her composure and model-walked her way over to her friends' tables. "I didn't realize it was kindergarten hour," she said, throwing a nonchalant eye-roll toward the offending tyke, like, *Can you believe some parents?*

"Point!" Alicia high-fived Massie as the boys smirk-nodded.

Massie sat down next to Landon.

"Vampire Weekend," Scott was saying to him, "is clearly the new Kings of Leon. I heard their concerts sell out in minutes. We have to go."

Landon smiled at Massie. Immediately, the tight knot in Massie's stomach loosened. What was it about the way Landon's ink-black hair fell over his glitter-nail-polish blue eyes that made her feel better than a full-body seaweed wrap? Even the fact that she would soon be living in a cardboard box didn't seem so bad, especially if she had Landon to bring her blankets from the Ralph Lauren Home collection and bottles of L'Occitane Verbena room spray.

"Have you heard the Comas?" said Luke, tucking his thick blond hair behind his ear. "They're the new Vampire Weekend."

"Actually they're the old Vampire Weekend," mock-scoffed Jackson, giving his friend a playful jab on the shoulder before helping himself to another slice of Garden Green pizza. Jackson was a strict vegetarian. "Frightened Rabbit is the new Vampire Weekend."

"Frightened Rabbit?" Alicia nibbled on the corner of a Margherita slice. "That sounds like a horror movie, not a band's name."

Dylan twitched her nose. "Th-th-th-th-th-that's all folks," she said, taking a bite of an imaginary carrot.

"Well, if you like Frightened Rabbit, then you should also listen to Aunt Martha," Scott said. Scott's first, second, and last love was DJ'ing, and he was always finding the newest of the new bands—the more obscure, the better.

Jackson just shook his head and threw a piece of tofu sausage at Luke. Within seconds, broccoli, pepperoni, and other such toppings were flying through the air.

"Food fiiiiiiiiiiiiight," Dylan burped.

Massie shook her head. Apparently boys in ninth weren't that much more mature than the Briarwood boys.

Kristen was staring at Massie, a strange look on her face. "Is everything okay?"

"Obviously," Massie said. In her head she whispered, *Not*.

Kristen squinted at her. "Are you sure? You look a little pale."

A wave of fear rippled up Massie's spine. Had Kristen been able to sniff out the poor on her? And the desperation that came from trying to hide it? Was it a *we can smell our own* kind of thing? Kristen, after all, had been poor for years before anyone found out. She clearly had a lot of practice in hiding it.

"I'm just worried the new Louis Vuitton messenger bag won't be released in time for the summer. I would hate to reuse last year's." Massie narrowed her eyes, daring Kristen to challenge the truthfulness of the statement, even though there was no LV messenger bag on the horizon.

"Oh, okay," Kristen said, looking unsure.

Massie breathed a sigh of relief. That was a close one. And

then she realized with a sudden stabbing pain that even if LV was developing a new messenger bag, she would not be able to buy it. She added it to the list of disappointments she'd been compiling since she had gotten the news.

Landon nudged Massie with his knee. Normally little butterflies spread out from the point of contact whenever Landon touched her, but poverty seemed to have numbed her to love. "Isn't that your friend?"

Massie turned just as Todd and Claire approached the counter. When Claire saw the PC, she waved vaguely. But when her eyes landed on Massie, her smile died and she turned sharply away. A wave of something passed through Massie. Maybe it was the whiff of spinach coming from the kitchen. Or maybe it was guilt over the way she'd treated Claire . . . and remorse over the fact that she couldn't take it back. Whatever it was, Massie took a big gulp of Alicia's Coke Zero to wash it down.

Todd marched over, a little navy wool cap pulled down over his little bald head. There was a lizard patch sewn in the middle. On his chest he wore a pin that had an angry X over a Santa face. Jagged letters spelled out SANTA'S DEAD. Massie's eye twitched with what felt suspiciously like guilt.

"You eating that?" he said pointing to the PC's last slice of deep-dish. "Don't mind if I do." He grabbed it and stuck the end in his mouth. As he chomped on his bite, a little string of cheese settled on his chin. "I'm going to need my strength if I'm going to redecorate Massie's room when my family moves into the Block estate."

Massie's heart lurched. Nine pairs of eyes turned toward her, pinning her in place.

"I'm thinking"—he chewed thoughtfully and tapped one finger against his grease-shiny lips—"wall-to-wall aquariums. A giant snake in one, maybe. And maybe one whole aquarium that's nothing but bugs. What do you think?" He looked at Massie as if he were really asking for her opinion.

Massie's lips felt glued together, and her Tory boots felt cemented to the floor. "What's he talking about?" Alicia said. Her chocolate-brown Ralph sweater perfectly complemented her brown eyes.

"Didn't she tell you?" Todd said, obviously enjoying the attention. He stood up a little straighter. "Massie's poor now."

Time stopped. It seemed like everyone in the pizza parlor had turned to look at Massie. The little six-year-old picked his nose and pointed his booger at her. Two high-schoolers at the next table over snickered behind their French manicures. The chef whispered something to the cashier, who burst out laughing. Claire stood at the counter, an unreadable expression on her makeup-less face.

"Poor?" Alicia laughed, looking at Massie. "That'll be the day."

Gawd, if you're listening, please make it stop! I promise to volunteer more if you just make Todd stop talking now.

Kristen's green eyes widened to the size of quarters, and she wiggled her fingers the way she usually did when she was excited.

"If you're looking for extra cash," Todd went on, "maybe you should think about selling your hair. You know, you could shave your head." He looked at her pointedly.

Massie tried to laugh. But it was no use. The world had begun to go blurry around the edges. She held on to her seat to keep from slipping under the table. She started to sweat in her very favorite, sequined peach Alice + Olivia sweater, which was especially awful because she could no longer afford to have it dry-cleaned. Just as she was wondering if she could fan her pits, she realized everyone was waiting for her response.

"He's probably just had too much Red Bull," said Massie finally. "He's hopped up on caffeine and hallucinating."

Todd shook his head. "It's you who's hallucinating, if you think your friends aren't going to find out that you're more broke than the Hubble telescope."

"He's lying," Dylan scoffed. "Right, Mass?"

"Right," Massie said. But she knew her voice sounded thinner than her now-canceled Visa. Kristen looked oddly excited.

"You think I'm lying? Ask my sister. Tell them, Claire," Todd called.

Everyone turned to Claire, who was fiddling with the Parmesan shaker at the condiment table. Massie wiped her palms on her jeans. The problem was, Claire *could* confirm Todd's story. And why wouldn't she, after what Massie had said to her? Massie would do it. For what felt like the twentieth time that day, Massie took an enormous breath and held it.

Massie's a horrible person, Claire would say, *and now she can't even afford to pay her friends to like her, like she did before.*

"Todd's right," Claire said, staring straight at Massie.

Bile rose in Massie's throat. *This was it.*

"She should sell her hair. She'd make a fortune. Not that she needs the money."

"Oh," said Kristen, looking kind of disappointed. "Then it's not true?"

Everyone at the table sat back, deflated. Claire walked to the table. "You know Todd, always scheming. He's been playing too much World of Warcraft, and his next target is the Block family."

"That's lame," Jackson said, crossing his skinny-jeaned legs.

"Yeah, not cool, man," Scott said, shaking his head.

Todd looked back and forth between Massie and Claire, as if he couldn't believed he'd been had by two girls who weren't even on speaking terms.

"Lyons!" called the clerk behind the counter. "Pizza's ready!"

Claire turned on the heels of her lime green Keds, claimed her pizza, and walked out. Todd trailed behind her, whispering angrily.

Massie swallowed, watching as Claire pushed the front door open and strutted outside. The Lyons' minivan was idling at the curb. Claire turned toward the window as she slipped inside, and in that moment, Massie realized something: Claire was beautiful. Not in a supermodel-with-eyelash-extensions kind of way. Not in a trying-hard, *The Hills* kind of way. Claire was beautiful in the way that belongs to people who know who they are.

Hot tears prickled at the back of Massie's eyes. The table had fallen back into happy chatter. The boys discussed more alterna-bands while Alicia, Dylan, and Kristen wondered when they would get another snow day.

"You okay?" Landon whispered.

"Bad pizza. I'll be right back." Massie slipped out of her seat and walked quickly back to the bathroom. Once in the stall, she pulled out her phone.

Massie: Thank U ☺.

The answer came back right away.

Claire: Truce?

In that moment, Claire's friendship meant more to Massie than any lost closet of couture.

Massie: Truce. C U @ home.

Massie sighed and held the phone close to her chest, wondering how much longer she'd be able to say that.

Only the strongest survive at Alpha Academy.
Who will be the Belle of the Brawl?

Turn the page for a sneak peek of Lisi Harrison's newest
novel in the #1 bestselling ALPHAS series . . .

1

"OHHMMMMM."

Sitting in full lotus position on a silver blue yoga mat, Charlie Deery's chapsticked lips formed a perfect circle as she chanted the sacred sound of the universe. But while her mouth was saying *om*, her mind was screaming *ommmhmuh-gud*. *Scared* had become the new sacred.

She opened one coffee-brown eye and peeked at Alpha Academy's holographic meditation yogi.

"No—ohhhhmmmm . . . peeking . . . ohmmmm," chanted Tran, his lids still blissfully shut. "Keeeep breathing . . . ohmmmmm."

The chubby monk—or "Chunk"—wore a flowing saffron robe and floated a few inches above the Zen Center's meditation pool. Conceived by Shira Brazille, head Alpha and creator of the academy's @-shaped island, Tran's purpose was to teach the girls at the fiercely competitive high school how to relax. And it was completely stressing Charlie out.

The meditation courtyard in the belly of the Buddha-shaped Zen Center should have been a calming respite, but after last night, Charlie wouldn't have been able to find peace at a Woodstock reunion. After one more deep inhalation of jasmine-scented air Charlie gave up.

"Sorry, Tran," she sighed, her mahogany bangs blowing up off her forehead. "I just can't focus."

Tran's puffy cheeks expanded with his smile, slicing his double chin into a quad. His eyes crinkled into crescents as his hologram face flickered out for a split-second and then reappeared. "Buddha says, 'The way is not in the sky. The way is in the heart.'"

"I don't even know which way is *up*," Charlie answered, her voice shaking with confusion and stirred with exhaustion. She had spent the night playing ref to an endless wrestling match between her heart and her brain, and still, there was no clear winner in sight.

She lifted her eyes to the patch of blue sky above the meditation courtyard. But instead of neon-colored parrots and personal airplanes, she saw a cloud-shaped Darwin and Allie, each silently imploring her to choose a side—their side.

"You are still looking outside yourself for answers, " he said, patting his virtual heart. "Look in."

"*How?*" Charlie asked, her sage-rage mounting.

Tran flickered again. He opened his mouth to speak, but she didn't want to hear it. The only thing Charlie wanted to "look in" was a pint of *Tell Me What To Do Before I Go Nuts* ice cream. Was he ever going to give her some *real* advice? If not, she'd be better off with a Magic Eight Ball. At least that gave answers.

"Namaste," she said, aiming her aPod at his muffin top, and pushing END SESSION.

"Namaste," he bowed and then disintegrated.

Now what?

She never should have let Shira connive her into breaking up with Darwin. She never should have convinced Allie to date him so she could keep tabs on him. She never should have confessed to Darwin that the dump was committed under duress. And she never should have stood there when he said he wanted her back. Because she had already promised him to Allie. But was he hers to promise?

Loyalty vs. Love? Head vs. Heart? BFFs vs. BFs? The answer was harder to come by than an iPad 4G.

Charlie unwound her legs from lotus position and reached toward the stone bench where she'd set down her breakfast, a frosted beaker full of a brain-stimulating protein shake specially concocted for invention majors. She placed the silver straw between her lips and took an aggressive sip. Hopefully the ice-cold green goo would cause brain freeze and grant her a moment of much-needed peace. But instead, all the green tea, ginger, and honey blend left behind was the metallic tinge of panic on her tongue and a mild stomachache.

Double now what?

Charlie pulled out her aPod again began pacing the perimeter of the meditation courtyard like a caged circus lion. She had one option left. Thumbing the screen she located the Alpha Class Selector app and started to scroll through her options to see what else she could add to her schedule. Overwhelmed by the 322 current courses, Charlie decided to start with the A's and quickly selected Acrobatics, Animation, Arabic, and Astronomy, bringing her total class periods up to eleven. Now she wouldn't have a spare second to fret about her life.

Time	Class	Location
7:30 a.m.	BREAKFAST AND MOTIVATIONAL LECTURE	Pavilion
8:00 a.m.	(RE)INVENTION (IM's ONLY) Mentored lab hour for Alpha experimentation, innovation, motivation.	Marie Curie Invention Laboratory
9:00 am	3-D RENDERING & ANIMATION Create, then replicate. Programs to reproduce your inventions on a global scale.	Melinda Gates Computer Lab
9:40 a.m.	INTRO TO ARABIC Prerequisite: Fluency in Spanish, French, and German.	Sculpture Garden

10:10 a.m.	PROTEIN BREAK Nourish your mind and body with a personalized smoothie. Drink fast. Your next class starts in ten minutues.	Health Food Court
10:20 a.m.	THE ART OF EXCELLENCE Betas work to live. Alphas live to work. Map your professional goals with a life coach and plot your path to the top.	Elizabeth I Lecture Hall
11:30 a.m.	HONE IT: FOR WRITERS Whether fact or fiction, when Alphas write, the world reads.	The Fuselage
12:40 p.m.	LUNCH AND SYMPHONY Digest lunch and life as you commune with Beethoven, Brahms and Tchaikovsky.	Pavilion
1:50 p.m.	GREENER PASTURES Learn how to keep your carbon footprint small while still wearing fabulous shoes.	Vertical Farm
2:55 p.m.	PHYSICS & QUANTUM LEAPS An Alpha in motion stays in motion. Advanced mechanical/philosophical investigations in matter and mind.	Newton's Apple Orchard
4:10 p.m.	ALPHAS THROUGH HISTORY Great women have always risen to the top. Follow their example!	Golda Meir Globe
5:10 p.m.	FIGURE DRAWING It's all in the details. Train your eye and your hands. The spirit will follow.	Sculpture Garden
6:00 p.m.	AERODYNAMIC TRAPEZE Soar to the top of your potential—Alphas dare to fly.	Achilles Track
8:00 p.m.	ASTRONOMY/ASTROLOGY Harness the constellations and reach for the stars.	Delphi Observatory

Setting her aPod down next to what remained of her breakfast, Charlie took a few cautious steps toward the reflection pool and leaned over until she could see herself in the placid water. She shivered and wrapped her arms around her bare shoulders, going over the situation for the hundredth time. Her relationships were tied in more knots than a cable-knit sweater. Wherever she pulled, she would end up with the same result: her life unraveling.

Charlie turned away from the pool and walked a few steps to the Zen garden, a rectangular patch of sand scattered with polished pink quartz and black obsidian rocks. Picking up a small rake, she began to scratch a list of pros and cons into the sand.

Stay True	Allie Who?
I have a best friend for the first time in my life—and I don't want to lose her.	Darwin is my soul mate. How can I pick a girl I just met over the boy I've loved my entire life?
Enrolling in Alpha Academy is all about making the most of myself. I need to impress Shira, not worry about Darwin!	But how can I be my best self without Darwin, the one person who makes me feel most confident and secure?
If Darwin and I are meant to be it will happen for us . . . someday. Why not let Allie be happy in the short term?	Wait! Darwin doesn't even like Allie. He likes me! Turning him down for Allie won't make a difference for their relationship.
Darwin and I are young. A break might be healthy.	Brakes are only good for one thing—screeching to a stop.

Charlie nibbled her cuticles and studied her list. One wrong yank and the fabric of her life would collapse.

"Buddha? What should I do?" Charlie shouted up through the cavity of the giant deity. Her low, sensible voice struck her as screechy and desperate as it echoed off the hammered-silver walls. "I need a sign. And I need it fast." She turned in a slow circle, like a satellite searching for a signal. A bird passed over the open sky above—was that the sign? Was it telling her to leave? Charlie bit her lip and struggled to interpret it, but it was so vague.

Ping!

A text from Buddha! How very modern.

She ran to her aPod.

Allie: Where R U? Hash browns at brkfst!

A slow smile spread across her face.

"Thanks, Buddha," Charlie whispered, stepping out into the tropical sunshine of Alpha Island. She yanked the elastic out of her ponytail and liberated her brown waves. She had her answer. She finally knew what to do.

The only question left was: could she go through with it?

2

APOD MESSAGE
TO ALL STUDENTS AND FACULTY
SUNDAY, SEPTEMBER 26TH
5:00 P.M.

FEEL THE BREEZE?

CHANGE IS IN THE AIR.

ASSEMBLY AT THE PAVILION.

6:00 P.M.

DON'T BE LATE!

—SHIRA

3

Hurrying down the gravel path between the dorms and the Pavilion, brushing past palm fronds, giant ferns, and fragrant plumeria, Allie A. Abbot's heart was soaring like the wings of the phoenix-shaped building in front of her.

Surrounded by Alphas in their school uniforms—clear gladiator sandals, balloon-sleeved button-down shirts, and pleated metallic miniskirts that twinkled in the twilight—Allie may not have been among friends, exactly, but at least she wasn't in disguise anymore. Her blond hair was back, navy blue eyes no longer hid behind fake green contact lenses, and she'd finally rebooted her golden tan. A beauty must-have she was forced to sacrifice while pretending to be Allie J. Abbott, the pasty eco-maniac who accused her of stealing sun from the flowers . . . along with her identity.

Unfortunately, the identity part was true. But oh, well. That was more behind her than the butt floss she proudly called underwear. The days of wearing recycled granny panties were over.

Over the past couple of months, Allie's self-esteem had congealed faster than food court Chinese food. The image of her boyfriend Fletcher, and best friend Trina, making out had been burned into the pleasure center of her brain. But now the burn was starting to scab over and Allie could put her energy toward scar-free healing. No more crying over the pieces of her broken heart. No more posing as Allie J. Abbot, the mega-famous folksinger whose acceptance letter she had accidentally received in the mail. No more black hair and bare feet. She had Charlie now. She had Darwin.

She had hope.

Read the rest of BELLE OF THE BRAWL,
coming October 2010.

And for more series secrets,
visit the Alphas online at
alphasacademy.com

The only thing harder than getting in is saying good-bye.

A TALE OF TWO PRETTIES

A CLIQUE NOVEL BY
#1 BESTSELLING AUTHOR LISI HARRISON

Ehmagawd, I just heard the juiciest gossip. This is the *final* CLIQUE novel!

Coming February 2011

poppy

www.pickapoppy.com

Welcome to Poppy.

A poppy is a beautiful blooming red flower (like the one on the spine of this book). It is also the name of the home of your favorite books.

Poppy takes the real world and makes it a little funnier, a little more fabulous.

Poppy novels are wild, witty, and inspiring. They were written just for you.

So sit back, get comfy, and pick a Poppy.

poppy